'Nicholas,' Eleanor said hastily, 'this is your Aunt Bridget. Say hello to her—like a gentleman.'

'Hello.' The warning in his mother's voice would be disregarded at his future peril and he knew it. Seven-year-old Nicholas produced his sweetest smile as added insurance.

Eleanor allowed herself to relax for a moment—perhaps it wasn't going to be so bad, after all. If Nicholas decided to behave . . . If Kevin would stop jittering . . .

Then she looked at her guest. Bridie was rigid with an emotion that might have been fear—but only partly fear. Fear, one could sympathize with and understand. It was the other emotion that repelled Eleanor.

Bridie's face was a mask of cold distaste. Her eyes, as she looked at Nicholas, were filled with a loathing she could not disguise. Eleanor knew then that this visitation was going to be far worse—far, far bloodier—than she had ever feared.

BY MARIAN BABSON

UNTIMELY GUEST

Marian Babson

BANTAM BOOKS
New York   Toronto   London   Sydney   Auckland

This edition contains the complete text
of the original hardcover edition.
Not one word has been omitted.

UNTIMELY GUEST

A Bantam Crime Line Book / published by arrangement with
St. Martin's Press

PRINTING HISTORY

First published in Great Britain by William Collins Sons & Co., Ltd.
St. Martin's edition published 1987
Bantam edition / January 1992

ISBN 0-553-29422-9

Published simultaneously in the United States and Canada

Printed in the United States of America

RAD   0 9 8 7 6 5 4 3 2 1

UNTIMELY GUEST

Prologue

There were screams, there were shouts, there were thuds—then silence.

She lay crumpled at the foot of the long steep stairs, her head and body twisted unnaturally.

The cries and exclamations of the others blurred into a flurry of incredulous noise as she tried to speak.

'Pushed me—' Her voice rose incredulously, although it seemed to tap her last reserves of energy to speak.

'*Pushed* me downstairs . . .'

The babble of noise rose again. 'Get an ambulance! . . . Quickly!' . . . 'Get a priest! . . . Hurry!' . . .

But her eyes closed, her last ghostly sigh was lost in the shock wave of the others' voices. She was dead.

Eleanor stared down at her unbelievingly, then slowly looked up the broad shadowed staircase rising at so steep a pitch behind the crumpled body.

It was dangerous—it had always been dangerous. More than once they had all remarked on that. But, somehow, it had never seemed deadly.

'. . . *pushed* . . .' Eleanor shook her head, trying to shake the memory of that faint voice from her mind, trying to deny the accusation she had heard. It was not possible.

It *could* not be possible. She looked round at the others. They were *family*. Not one of them could have— And yet, the woman lay dead at her feet.

'Accident . . .' someone was saying. Of course. That *had* to be the explanation. Most accidents happen in the home.

So do most murders.

It was not possible—not one of *them*. They had their quarrels. What family hadn't? All right, perhaps there had been, of late, more than the normal family disagreements. Perhaps the basic tenets of family life, of faith, even of love, *had* been mocked and threatened. But normal people faced problems like that and solved them without resorting to . . . to *this*.

It could not be true. The accusation had been the product of a mind sliding away from mortality to the infinite. A last despairing protest against the fate that had so suddenly overtaken it. One could understand that.

One could not understand—could not encompass—murder.

Yet, even as she tried to convince herself of the reasonable explanation, part of Eleanor's consciousness traitorously speculated about the possibility of the other. (They were not her *own* family, her mind insinuated, they were her husband's family. And, God knew, they all had their oddities.)

But this?

Not this, her conscious brain insisted. *Not this*.

Oddities, yes. Bitter quarrels, certainly. Family feuds, even. But this?

How could things have come to *this* pass?

1.

To begin with, there were the questions—not one of which she could, hand on heart, answer with any degree of certitude.

'Will she have any hair?' Nicholas kept asking urgently during the long days of waiting. At seven, certain questions acquired an importance disproportionate to their intrinsic value. Part of it, Eleanor suspected, was based on their annoyance quotient to adult figures of authority. 'Will she have any hair at all?'

'Don't be silly, Nicholas.' A calm tone, an unruffled appearance—try to minimize the situation, make it appear part of the normal flow of life. 'Of course she will.' (Dear God, *would* she?)

'But how much hair will she have?' Nicholas persisted. 'And will it be real hair, like yours? Or will it be just all stubby, like Daddy when he needs a shave?'

'Go and wash your hands. We'll be eating soon.'

'Mickey Concannon says she'll be bald as an egg. He says that's why girls go in to begin with—so that nobody will notice.'

'Wash your hands!'

Kevin, thirty years older than Nicholas—but not, apparently, old enough to know better—began on his own leitmotiv as he came through the door.

'How long is she going to stay?'

'How should I know? You read the only letter she sent. You know as much about it as I do.'

'I'm sorry.' His contrition didn't extend to changing the subject. 'If only we had some idea of her plans. Do you think she's going to be here a few days? A few weeks? She couldn't think we mean her to move in permanently, could she?'

'I don't know.'

'I wonder, was it wise? I know we've got the spare room, but—?'

It's always fatal to decide upon the last thing one ought to say to a loved one in any given situation. When that situation arises, there's the thing right on the tip of your tongue. She heard herself hurl it at him now.

'She's *your* sister!'

'I know, I know.' He was immediately defensive, taking it as a criticism. 'But she couldn't go home. Veronica has enough to cope with. We'll be lucky if this doesn't kill Mam, as it is. She'll never be able to understand.'

Her father had gone on private record, at the stormy time of their wedding, with his opinion that Mam was a woman you couldn't kill with a meat-axe. But it was not the sort of remark calculated to endear a daughter-in-law, if repeated.

'Times are changing,' she temporized. 'Mam will just have to learn that.'

'Ah,' he shook his head. 'But *will* she?'

The telephone saved her from having to answer that one.

'Hello? Ellie, is that you?' Carmel's voice came bubbling over the wire.

'Hello, Carmel.' Eleanor resisted the temptation to say, '*No, it's Bridie,*" and hear Carmel's gasp of consternation.

'Has she come yet?' The conspiratorial tone was

somehow out of place when one considered that Carmel phoned at least three times a day to ask the same question.

'I told you I'd ring you when she arrived.' That, too, had been said many times before.

'I know. But she might have just come and you might not have been able to get to the phone yet.' Carmel's life was a succession of improbable speculations, none the less real to her for being engendered by the magic word 'might'. Anything *might* happen. Perhaps it helped to insure her to the fact that all that *did* happen—with monotonous regularity—was pregnancy.

'Well, she hasn't.'

'Do you suppose she might have changed her mind?'

'That would be too much to hope for.' The best thing about Carmel was that one could be honest with her and know that she'd understand. Outwardly unlike, Eleanor and Carmel had a bond no man could put asunder—they had both married into the same family. Consequently, they were the only members of it capable of standing back and watching with some degree of detachment when internecine warfare threatened to overwhelm all up to and including the third degree of kinship.

'I thought I might come round later—if you're going to be home.'

'I'll be here,' Eleanor agreed, ringing off. Carmel had learned as much as she had called to find out.

Passing the highchair in which Margaret perched docilely chewing a rusk, Eleanor caressed the soft feathery curls. It would be months yet before Margaret learned to talk. She was literally incapable of asking questions. At the moment, that made her Eleanor's favourite member of the family.

Upstairs, the spare room waited. Eleanor stood in the doorway, checking it automatically. (What did she expect to find? That Bridie had moved in unnoticed and taken up residence?)

Tomorrow the flowers would need changing. She knew that Kevin thought it a useless gesture to keep the vases filled in an empty room, but she could not bear the thought that Bridie might arrive without any further warning and find no slightest sign of welcome waiting for her. Bridie had so little to come back to.

She moved into the room, hovering irresolutely. Did it look all right? The mirror—should it really be in the room at all? There was already one mirror—part of the dressing-table—was the second one, hanging on the wall, too much? But, if she took it down, she had nothing to replace it and the long narrow swatch of unfaded wallpaper would proclaim what was missing as surely as if it had been labelled. Mirrors have such a distinctive shape.

But the Victorian *prie-dieu* squatting against the farther wall was the basic source of her uneasiness. Should she—she went over the familiar ground again—leave it in the room? Would Bridie take it as some sort of personal comment? Or, if she moved it out into the hall, would Bridie bring it back in here?

It was the sort of small problem that had grown to enormous size and insolubility during the past few days. (Kevin didn't know. 'Heavens, don't ask *me*,' Carmel had shuddered. Veronica had withdrawn so far into the fastnesses of her own life and troubles that it seemed unkinder to risk upsetting her than upsetting Bridie.)

Eleanor closed her eyes, trying to recall Bridie to mind, but it had been ten years ago. She had just started going with Kevin and his family were still shadowy figures in the distance whom it might not be necessary for her ever to meet. He hadn't even talked about them much. Not until that sudden upsurge of drama, during which one sister ran away with another's fiancé, their father died in pursuit of the elopers, and the jilted sister retreated completely from a life which had become too much for her. (Kevin had reluctantly imparted the information, obviously feeling that his wife-to-be was going to have to know a few things about the family.)

It was about the same time that Patrick had proposed to Carmel, and the weddings of the two sons, following so closely on one another, had tended to obscure the earlier drama. Besides, Bridie had been so neatly—fittingly—out of the way by then that she was regarded by most of the family as having almost decently been buried. Who would have imagined that she would snap back into life again all these years later?

Eleanor moved the *prie-dieu* away from the wall, setting it beside the bed. Did it look more like an ordinary chair there? (It didn't look in any way *reproachful*, did it?) She might have put it somewhere else, but it had always been in the guest-room and Nicholas would be sure to comment upon it— unfailingly at the wrong moment. (Could there be any *right* moment?) Or Bridie might see it, wherever she put it, and to have such a chair in the house, but not in Bridie's room, would seem more pointed than leaving it here.

The doorbell rang—that would be Carmel. With a final desperate glare at the *prie-dieu*, Eleanor pushed it slightly askew (as though a more rakish angle might somehow disguise it) and hurried downstairs.

There was a howl from the kitchen as she reached the foot of the stairs.

'Mother—' Nicholas's indignant bellow filled the hallway. 'Margaret threw her milk at me. It's all over the floor.'

'And what did you do to her to—?' Eleanor flung the front door ajar in passing, bellowing back preparatory to joining battle in the kitchen. It was highly unlikely that Margaret had deliberately thrown her

milk at Nicholas. It was far more likely that she had
spilled it, or that he had knocked it over teasing her.
That the milk was all over the floor was the only point
in his statement she didn't doubt.

Almost to the kitchen, she halted. There were no
following footsteps—as there would have been had
Carmel entered. And, come to think of it, the brief
glimpse she had had of the slight form in the doorway
had shown no resemblance to Carmel.

'Oh God!' She did an abrupt about-face and re-
traced her steps.

The figure stood waiting, eyes cast down, hands
folded at waist, the two suitcases at her side nearly as
big as she was—certainly a lot bulkier.

'*Do* come in!' Eleanor opened the door wide. 'I'm
so sorry, I thought it was— I mean, I wasn't expecting— Come in—' (*What* did one call her?)

'No, please—' As the slight figure stooped to take
up the suitcases, Eleanor stopped her. 'Kevin will see
to those.' She raised her voice above the din coming
from the kitchen. 'Kevin! KE-vin!'

Then he was behind her, uneasy, cued by the faint
note of hysteria in her voice.

'Bridie!' He put his hand out, then seemed to
realize that that was a bit too formal a greeting for a
sister.

As Bridie, with delayed reaction, unclasped her
hands and started to hold one out, Kevin bobbed to
plant a kiss on her cheek. They collided awkwardly.

'The cases,' Eleanor said.

'Of course.' Kevin gathered them up, grateful for
something to do. 'Of course. I'll take them upstairs.'
He escaped thankfully.

The uproar in the kitchen had not abated. Margaret had begun to cry and Nicholas was issuing a
lurid up-to-the-second bulletin at the top of his lungs
every thirty seconds.

'Mother—Margaret's got a puddle of milk on her

tray and she's hitting it with her hand . . . Mother—
she's splattering it everywhere! . . . Mother—Margaret's
making faces at me . . . Mother—Margaret's crying!'

'I know. We can hear her.' Eleanor fought down
the temptation to go and smack them both. Why did
children always play up as soon as guests arrived? She
glanced at Bridie sympathetically, ready to meet her
eyes with a rueful shrug.

Bridie's eyes remained resolutely downcast, but she
could not hide a flinch as she crossed the doorstep
and the din from the kitchen engulfed her.

Bridie would just have to get used to it, Eleanor
decided. At that, it was several decibels below the
racket produced when any of Carmel's brood joined
her own. Bridie would never again, in all likelihood,
find a place as quiet as the place she had left. Bridie
would simply have to adjust—toughen up—every-
body else in the world.

An inhospitable little thought—perhaps triggered
off by the spring in Kevin's step as he bounded up the
stairs—snaked through her mind. If Bridie found the
atmosphere uncongenial here, perhaps she wouldn't
stay long.

Poor Bridie, Eleanor reproached herself instantly.
After all she must have been through. How can you—?

'Mother!' Unable to raise any satisfactory response to
his urgent bellowing, Nicholas charged into the hallway
to see what the rival attraction was. He stopped short,
staring at Bridie. 'Oh!'

Eleanor was profoundly grateful that Bridie *did*
have hair. A bit short, perhaps, but *there*. Not that that
would necessarily prevent Nicholas from comment-
ing just the same.

'Nicholas,' she said hastily, before he got his breath
back. 'This is your Aunt Bridget. Say hello to her—like
a gentleman.'

'Hello.' The warning in his mother's voice would be

disregarded at his future peril and he knew it. He produced his sweetest smile as added insurance.

Eleanor allowed herself to relax for a moment—perhaps it wasn't going to be so bad, after all. If Nicholas decided to behave . . . If Kevin would stop jittering . . .

Then she looked at her guest. Bridie was rigid with an emotion that might have been fear—but only partly fear. Fear, one could sympathize with and understand. It was the other emotion that repelled Eleanor.

Bridie's face was a mask of cold distaste. Her eyes, as she looked at Nicholas, were filled with a loathing she could not disguise. Perhaps she realized this; she lowered her lids quickly, nodded to a dismayed Nicholas, and stood there in a meek submissive pose which could fool no one who had suddenly had a glimpse of the cauldron bubbling just below the surface.

Eleanor knew then that this visitation was going to be far worse—far, far bloodier—than she had ever feared.

2.

One goes on. No matter how disquieting the intuitions and insights vouchsafed by unguarded moments, the essential elements of social life must prevail.

'The guest-room is upstairs.' Ridiculously, Eleanor felt safer in directing Bridie's attention from Nicholas. (What harm could she do him? Why should she wish to do him any harm? Where had these terrifying thoughts come from?)

'Upstairs—' Eleanor stepped back, forcing Bridie to precede her up the stairs, feeling another small triumph at having won in even so faint a clash of wills, at putting herself between Bridie and Nicholas.

'The end door on the right.' It was the only door open, Bridie was heading for it anyway. 'It's quieter at the back and the garden is quite pretty in the spring— it's not at its best right now, I'm afraid.'

(Dear God—did that imply that she thought Bridie might still be there to see it in the spring? Why couldn't she stop talking? Why was she babbling on so? Was it, perhaps, because silence was—had been— Bridie's chosen *métier*? Did she feel she was keeping Bridie at some necessary disadvantage by not allowing her the silence she must need in order to compose her thoughts and correlate all the new impressions that must be crowding in on her?)

Kevin had placed one of the suitcases on the seat of the *prie-dieu*, ready to be opened, and draped a coat over the back. That took care of that problem for the moment—it looked a bit sawed-off at the legs, perhaps, but like an ordinary chair.

'I hope you'll find this comfortable, Bridie,' Kevin said. (Why did he always have to sound pompous when he was most unsure of himself?) 'You ought to. Eleanor's worked hard fixing it up for you.'

'Thank you,' Bridie said tonelessly. 'You're very kind.'

'We're your family,' Kevin said. 'Kindness doesn't come into it. You're home.'

Bridie dipped her head in a dutiful submission to a pronouncement from a higher authority. It seemed to embarrass Kevin even more.

'We'll leave you to pull yourself together—' He broke off, perhaps realizing that it wasn't the most tactful of remarks. 'Sort yourself out—' That sounded no better.

'We'll be downstairs,' Eleanor said firmly. 'Come down and have a cup of tea when you're ready.'

'You're very kind,' Bridie murmured again.

They closed the door behind them with, Eleanor felt, equal relief. Kevin's forehead was filmed with perspiration.

'God!' he said. 'I don't know how long we can stand this.'

'She's just feeling a bit strange.' Eleanor tried to offer a comfort she did not quite believe in. 'After a couple of days, she'll be more relaxed—'

'Bridie was always a bit strange,' Kevin said thoughtfully. 'And I don't think it's done her any good—being where she's been.'

It was the kind of statement that could lead to an

argument, whether agreed or disagreed with. Eleanor prudently kept silence.

In the kitchen, the children were oddly subdued. Margaret dabbled her fingers in the pool of milk filling the tray of her high chair. Nicholas crouched at the foot of the chair, sailing a miniature paper boat in the overflow pool of milk down there. Furface, the cat (Nicholas had been allowed to name her), was busily licking away at the other end of the puddle, ignoring the fact that she had a saucerful of perfectly good milk under the stove.

Neither of the children seemed particularly aware that their parents had just entered and Eleanor silently began the mopping-up operations, as abstracted as they. Kevin slumped into a chair at the table, picked up a fork and began tracing mysterious hieroglyphics in the butter. It was no mystery where the children had inherited their tendencies. However, it was not the moment to mention people giving bad examples by playing with food.

The silence in the kitchen stretched out unnaturally. There was nothing companionable about it. Rather, it had a listening quality, as though even the baby were straining her ears to catch any sounds from overhead. But there was nothing to hear. Bridie made no more noise than a disembodied spirit.

The back door opened abruptly, causing them all to jump. Carmel edged inside, looking around carefully before she spoke.

'The light's on upstairs in the guest-room. Is she—?'

'Yes,' Eleanor said. 'She's here.'

'And—?' Carmel stared upwards, as though she might spy through the floor.

'And what?' Kevin asked irritably. 'She's here. What more do you expect?'

'Oh.' Carmel exchanged a *'So it's like that, is it?'* glance with Eleanor.

'Sit down,' Eleanor said. The kettle had begun to boil. 'Have a cup of tea.'

'Gladly.' Carmel lowered her bulk into the nearest chair. At eight-months-odd along, she preferred to get off her feet whenever she had the chance—which wasn't often with her brood.

The silence descended again. Carmel semaphored wildly with her eyebrows and Eleanor replied with a meaning glance at the children. As an afterthought, she included Kevin in the glance. Carmel nodded and settled back.

Eleanor made the tea, wondering whether Bridie had eaten on the train, or whether she should be offered a meal—however makeshift—now. Instinct told her that Bridie, if asked, would claim that she had eaten in order not to be any trouble. On the other hand, it would be a form of intrusion, if not cruelty, to go bursting in on her with a tray, insisting she eat, when she really might have eaten on the train—at least, eaten as much as she wanted. One had the impression that food was not very important to Bridie.

Unlike Carmel. 'Any biscuits going?' she enquired eagerly.

It was a question after Nicholas's own heart. He dashed to help, taking the box of biscuits from Eleanor's hand and conveying it to Carmel's.

'Thank you, Nicholas.' While she was opening the packet, Nicholas abruptly threw himself upon as much lap as she had available.

'I want to go home with you.' His voice was muffled against her knees, but the words were clear enough in the silent room.

'Oh, Nicholas,' Carmel stroked his head. 'What's the matter? Has—'

'It might not be such a bad idea.' Eleanor was surprised at the gratitude with which she clutched at the suggestion. 'If you could manage, Carmel, just for a night or two, until things settle down—'

'Ellie! For God's sake!' Kevin's irritation exploded.

'Just until Bridie gets a little more settled—' Eleanor refused to be shouted down. 'She isn't used to having children around.'

'There are a lot of things Bridie isn't used to.' Kevin's jaw set stubbornly. 'But she can start getting used to them. Let's get one thing straight—this house isn't going to be run to suit Bridie! She chose to come here and she can take us as we are, or—'

'Oh!' The gasp from the doorway choked him off in full flow.

They turned in time to see Bridie whirl and dash away, making no more sound than she had when appearing there.

'Oh God!' Kevin groaned. 'Go after her, will you, Ellie?'

'She's *your* sister.' This time it was Carmel who said it.

'Yes, but, another woman—'

'Women don't have that much in common,' Carmel said. *Especially with Bridie,* was implicit in her tone.

'I know—' Kevin gestured helplessly. 'But—'

'It's all right.' Bridie was back in the doorway. (How were they going to live with someone who could creep around without making a sound? They'd never dare start an unguarded conversation again, much less make any critical remarks or have a row. Was this an end to all privacy, all naturalness?)

'It's my fault.' Bridie sidled into the room, eyes downcast. 'Kevin is right—you mustn't change anything because of me. It's so kind of you to have me— I don't want to be a burden to you.'

'Oh, Bridie—' Now Kevin was red-faced and floundering. (Had Bridie always had this effect on him?)

'No, no. You must tell me the instant I'm in your

way,' Bridie said, thus effectively cutting off any possibility that they might actually do so.

'This is your home, Bridie,' Kevin insisted. (For someone who had been so worried about the length of Bridie's stay, he was now doing his best to ensure that she felt she need never leave.) Eleanor exchanged a helpless glance with Carmel.

'You're looking well, Bridie,' Carmel said blandly, dragging the emotional temperature down from an overheated stratosphere.

'Ohh—' For a moment Bridie looked as though she might deny it. 'Thank you—and you're—' Her eyes came up briefly and scanned Carmel's enormous bulge. Her face flamed and her eyes dropped away as though they had encountered the obscene.

'Tea, Bridie?' Eleanor hastily slammed down a cup and saucer before Carmel could say anything. Carmel's own face had gone red and there was a dangerous glint in her eyes.

'More, Carmel?' The teapot hovered over her cup.

'Indeed, yes. I'm drinking for two, you know.' Carmel shot a challenging glare across the table. 'You're going to be an aunt, Bridie—again.'

'I won't have any more,' Kevin refused tea hastily.

'I wish *my* husband would say that.' Carmel was not to be diverted. 'You got the only reasonable member of the family, Eleanor.'

Bridie's face was deep red, her hand shaking as she lifted the teacup to her lips, trying to ignore the innuendoes around her.

Poor Bridie—Eleanor felt a momentary compunction—it was a far cry from a quiet convent. And she shouldn't be subjected to a family fight on her first night home. Although, fairness to Carmel compelled Eleanor to admit, Bridie had brought it on herself.

'I'll give Nicholas his bath now.' Kevin recklessly volunteered for a job he had seldom tackled and never alone.

'I don't want a bath.' Nicholas made perfunctory protest.

'I didn't ask you what you wanted.' Kevin strode around the table, grasped Nicholas's arms and heaved him firmly up on to his shoulders. Nicholas dissolved in laughter, gripping Kevin's hair tightly.

'Giddy-up,' he ordered.

Kevin obligingly neighed, and broke into a run, thundering down the hallway and up the stairs. They left the impression in their wake of being delighted to escape and leave the kitchen to the possession of the women.

Eleanor took her own cup of tea and retreated to stand beside the high chair. Somehow, she felt she wanted to stay poised for action. Margaret cooed happily and reached out for her. Eleanor patted Margaret's head absently.

'That's Margaret?' Bridie appeared to find an already-arrived baby far less embarrassing than an impending one. 'How old is she now?'

'Eleven months,' Eleanor said.

'Eleven months . . .' Bridie murmured, and they seemed to lose her again as she retreated inward, possibly remembering her own life eleven months ago when all had been peaceful with no hint of the storms to come.

Or had it been so peaceful? Surely this sort of thing couldn't have arrived out of thin air—there must have been warnings, rumours, discontents, suspicions. Even the most cloistered convent could not close out all threat of impending disruption—not on such a scale . . .

Abruptly, Eleanor shivered. *Someone's walking over my grave.* A ridiculous saying, really, and one she hadn't thought of in years. No reason why it should return to her now.

Yes, there was: face it. Bridie had brought the aura of another world with her. Suddenly one was aware of all manner of things it would be preferable to forget. Things that had, in fact, been forgotten for the past ten years.

Bridie set down her cup. 'Thank you,' she said, without looking up. 'That was very nice. You're very kind.'

Teeth on edge, Eleanor forced a smile. 'Wouldn't you like something else—?'

The tap at the back door might have passed unnoticed in the usual brisk bustle of life in the house—a life the loss of which Eleanor found she was already beginning to mourn. In the newly-initiated reign of silence, it rang clear and loud as Gabriel's horn. Even Bridie looked up, startled, to see what it portended.

Veronica bolted into the room, letting the door slam behind her. She had tossed an oatmeal-coloured cardigan over her shoulders and was out of breath from her short dash the length of the street from Mam's big house on the corner. A gust of cold air swept in with her and seemed to surround her like a cloud. She shivered in the midst of it.

'Oh God! Isn't this all we need right now?' Her glasses misted over, unable to distinguish faces on the dimly-seen figures in the kitchen, she blurted out her news.

'Dee-Dee's back!'

3.

Bridie pushed back her chair and ran from the room. Stricken, Veronica stared after her vaguely.

'Who's that?'

'That was Bridie,' Eleanor said. 'She arrived about an hour ago.'

'Oh God!' Too late, Veronica snatched off her glasses and mopped at them with a loose-hanging cardigan sleeve.

'That's bloody torn it,' Carmel said. 'It lacked only this.'

'Oh, well.' Veronica replaced her glasses and seemed to see a silver lining. 'At least she didn't wait to hear the worst.'

'My God!' Carmel gasped. 'There's more?'

'Dee-Dee's brought a man home with her.' Veronica's voice lowered conspiratorially and she glanced towards the doorway. 'She's calling him her fiancé.'

'Never!' Carmel's eyes glistened. 'What does Mam say?'

'She doesn't know yet. That's why I can't stay. I just popped over to tell you,' Veronica hitched the cardigan more firmly around her shoulders. 'I ought to be getting back.'

'Have a cup of tea first,' Eleanor said, automatically pouring one.

'But what about Terence?' Carmel asked eagerly. 'Where is he? Does *he* know yet?'

'He's on the road.' Veronica perched on the edge of a chair, reaching for her tea. 'But he'll be home tomorrow night and he'll have to stay all week. It's their big week at headquarters. There's some big product launch coming up and there'll be demonstrations and sales conferences all week. And then there's the Annual Dinner on Saturday. He'll have to be there all through it.'

'That will keep *him* out of the way, then,' Carmel comforted. 'You know these big sales conferences— and they'll be having to entertain out-of-town bigwigs afterwards. He'll never know she's around—if nobody tells him.'

'He'll be hard put to miss her.' A trace of grimness shaded Veronica's tone. 'She's staying at the house. *And* she's insisting on the guest-room for her—her— James.'

'Mam will have a fit!' Carmel could not keep the glee out of her voice. 'She'll never stand for that!'

'She's going to have to.' Veronica looked unexpectedly militant. She was usually so put-upon that they tended to forget she had a determination and a temper of her own. 'It's *my* house and I'm not throwing my own sister out of it—no matter what Mam says!'

In the face of this declaration, there was a brief startled silence. It was true that the house belonged to Veronica. In a burst of unsuspected acumen, her father had willed it to her, reserving the right for Mam to occupy it for the remainder of her life, if she so desired. The terms of the will had come as a considerable shock to Mam (although she had money of her own)—to all of them, in fact. They'd never thought the old man possessed that much insight.

(Had Veronica been so plainly marked as the family victim, even then? Or had her father realized, earlier than the others, that Mam had determined upon Veronica as the mainstay of her old age—never mind what it did to Veronica's own life—and done the little he could to try to give Veronica some faint protection against the icy winds that might blow in the years to come?)

Nevertheless, it was so seldom Veronica asserted her rights that the shock of it alone was often enough to carry the battle for her. Especially as everyone in the family had a lurking sense of guilt about her being left to shoulder the burden of caring for Mam.

'Do you think—' Veronica cast a worried glance upwards—'I ought to go up and say hello? I mean, it seems so cold just to—' She seemed to shrink into herself, not completing the sentence.

'I wouldn't,' Carmel absolved her quickly. 'Leave Bridie alone to get her feet under her. She'll be more herself in the morning. She's had as much as she can cope with today.'

So has Veronica. Eleanor met Carmel's eyes and the unspoken message passed between them.

'Yes, perhaps you're right,' Veronica agreed thankfully. 'Everything will look better in the morning.'

If she could convince herself of that, she was the prize optimist of all time. But only an optimist could bear to live with Mam.

'I ought to be getting home.' Veronica sounded doubtful, perhaps thinking of the scenes that still lay ahead.

'I'll walk you back.' Carmel heaved herself to her feet.

Upstairs, shrieks of laughter and noisy splashes were coming from the bathroom. The baby began slapping her hand down on her tray in gleeful reminiscence of the unguarded minutes when there had been a lovely pool of milk there.

'I'll call you first thing in the morning,' Carmel

assured Eleanor unnecessarily. She usually did, even when there was no family crisis in the offing.

'Fine,' Eleanor said mechanically, catching Margaret's hand and restraining her.

'Come down for coffee, why don't you?' Veronica invited. 'Nicholas will be at school and you can bring the baby along. Mam always likes to see babies.'

'Don't I know it!' Carmel said. She caught up her coat and slipped it over her shoulders while Veronica held the door for her, letting another blast of cold air into the kitchen.

'Good night, then, and take it easy,' Carmel said. She and Veronica went down the path and turned out of sight.

The baby began to grizzle and, sighing faintly, Eleanor picked her up and comforted her.

'Ellie?' Kevin stood in the doorway, triumphant from the damp tendrils curling over his forehead to the tips of his sopping shoelaces. 'I put Nicholas to bed.'

'Wonderful!' Eleanor applauded. With enough encouragement, he might even do it again some time.

'I thought—' He moved into the kitchen, looking round. 'I thought I heard Veronica's voice.'

'She was here.' He would have to know, sooner or later. 'She came to tell us Dee-Dee's back.'

'Oh!' He sat down abruptly, as though his legs had folded under him. 'What a time for her to come back!'

'Yes.' Eleanor transferred the baby to his arms and began to clear the table.

'What do you think she's come back *for?*'

'It sounds—' Eleanor checked quickly to make sure he had a firm grip on the baby. 'It sounds as though she decided the time had come to introduce her new fiancé to the family. She's brought him with her.'

'Fiancé?' Blank-faced, he dandled the baby absently. 'You can't mean she's thinking of getting married?'

'That's usually what a fiancé implies.'

'But—' He grappled with the thought. 'What about Terence?'

'What about him?' They were heading for one of their direct confrontations, there was no way of escaping it.

'Dee-Dee's married to *him*.'

'Not any more.' As soon as the laws had been relaxed, Dee-Dee had applied on the grounds of 'irretrievable breakdown'. Terence would never have divorced her and, before that, her only hope would have been a plea of 'desertion', but that would not have worked—Terence would have followed her anywhere. 'The divorce was granted years ago.'

'That doesn't make any difference.'

'It does in the eyes of the Law.'

'In the eyes of God, they're still married. Dee-Dee knows that. She can't marry anyone else.'

'No?' If Dee-Dee had not had the idea of an eventual remarriage at the back of her mind, she would not have bothered to sort out her legal position. But Kevin, blinkered about equally by Mam and her Church, had always refused to face certain facts.

'Oh, it's different for you, I know. You're a Protestant. You don't understand—'

'Perhaps not.' She understood that Mam had been holding Terence as a permanent lodger by filling him with promises of a repentant Dee-Dee remembering her upbringing at last and returning to the marriage bed. The fact that, like every victim of a confidence racket, Terence had been a willing accomplice to his own deception, did not make it less blameworthy.

'Poor Terence.' Kevin sighed heavily. 'This will be a terrible blow to him. Unless—' he brightened— 'Mam can make Dee-Dee see reason.'

Eleanor attacked the dirty dishes, not trusting herself to speak.

'Oh, I know what you think,' Kevin accused. 'But

you're wrong. Dee-Dee may have got into the ways of
the world and lapsed. But at heart—and back at
home, among her own kind—'

'What I was *actually* thinking,' Eleanor said crisply,
'was that we shouldn't be discussing this so loudly.
Have you forgotten Bridie's upstairs?'

'Oh my God!' He had. He deflated slowly, becoming a man with too many sisters whose behaviour was
utterly beyond him. 'What are we going to do?'

'I don't see that we have to do anything. Everyone
concerned is over twenty-one—well over. If they can't
sort out their own lives—'

'It's not that simple.' It never was, of course.
Especially among tightly-knit Irish families. Kevin
stood and began to pace the floor. Margaret burbled
her approval of this turn of events.

'God! That Dee-Dee should choose now, of all
times, to come back. With Bridie just here and—'

'Has it occurred to you—' the thought had been
with Eleanor for what seemed like days now and she
felt a faint relief at sharing it—'that that may be why
Dee-Dee's come back? It's too much of a coincidence,
otherwise.'

'But why?' Kevin sat down again, stricken. 'Why
should Dee-Dee do that?'

It had to be a rhetorical question. If Kevin hadn't
fathomed his own sisters after a lifetime, how could
he expect a mere sister-in-law, who had hardly met
them, to explain them?

Eleanor dried the last cup and put it away, then
took the baby from Kevin's arms.

'Bath time,' she said. 'And then bed.' It was hours
past the baby's bedtime now, but she still didn't seem
sleepy. With luck, she'd sleep late in the morning.

Morning—Eleanor's mind tested the word and
flinched away. She found that she really did not wish
to think about tomorrow.

Margaret bathed and put into her cot, Eleanor

checked on Nicholas and found him sleeping soundly, although his forehead was rumpled by a frown as though, even in sleep, he was puzzling over an unsatisfactory question and trying to find an acceptable answer.

Across the corridor, a thin slash of light rimmed Bridie's door—she was still awake then. Bracing herself, Eleanor tapped on the door.

The light instantly disappeared, the door remained obdurately closed. Eleanor had the curious sensation that, behind it, Bridie crouched defensively like an animal tracked to its lair and cowering from the hunter.

'It's just me,' Eleanor called. (Although heaven knew who else Bridie might be expecting. Perhaps a tap on the door such as she had given was a warning signal, or reproach, in the convent.) 'Is everything all right? Is there anything else you'd like?'

'Thank you . . . no.' After a long time, the answer came, faint and indistinct.

'I'll say goodnight, then,' Eleanor told the closed door. (Why should she feel that, if she tried to open it, she would find that a chair had been braced beneath the knob?) 'I hope you sleep well.'

'Thank you . . .' Even fainter, as though Bridie were fading away and tomorrow there would be only an uneasy memory to mark her passage. 'You're . . . very kind.'

'It may not be so bad, you know.' Kevin, ensconced in bed with a glass of Scotch, a magazine, and the evening paper, had obviously been cheering himself into a mood of incautious optimism. 'I can't imagine she'll want to stay here long, with the kids and all. She'll want to look for some place quieter. And she'll want to find herself a job, start making some money—'

Undressing quietly, Eleanor simply raised an eyebrow at that idea.

'Well, of course,' Kevin said. 'I know she hasn't shorthand or typing. But there are lots of jobs girls can do without that. You can see the ads—' he tossed the newspaper to the floor, following it with the magazine—'all over the place. A minimum of training, that's all, and there are all the opportunities in the world.'

Of course there were. Selling encyclopedias, croupier in a gambling club, start your own cosmetic business—the opportunities were endless. And Bridie could be expected to be so enthusiastic about any one of them.

'I'll mention it to her in the morning,' Kevin said expansively. He drained his glass and set it on the bedside table.

'You do that,' Eleanor agreed, slipping her nightgown over her head.

'Or perhaps we ought to be subtler—' Bridie and second thoughts seemed to go together, Eleanor had already noted.

'Yes,' Kevin decided. 'I won't actually *say* anything. We'll just leave the newspapers around turned to the Situations Vacant pages. And maybe not tomorrow. We'll give her a few days to settle down first.'

'You can try.' Eleanor snapped off the light and slipped into bed and into his waiting arms.

'Ah, let's forget the whole thing for tonight.' His arms tightened around her, one hand plucked at the shoulder strap of her nightgown. 'What did you bother with that thing for, anyway?'

'You didn't say anything.' She snuggled down closer.

'Well, you might have—' He broke off, raising his head to listen. 'What's that?'

'What?' Eleanor raised her own head, and then she

heard it. The choking, racking sobs penetrated even through closed doors and along the corridor.

'It's not one of the kids?' Kevin's voice betrayed that he didn't really believe it was.

'No.' No child could reach such a pitch of anguish and despair. They were the sobs of an adult, of a soul that believed itself lost and turned out of paradise, away from the only home it knew or desired.

'Should we go to her?' Kevin asked uncertainly.

'I don't think so.' Bridie would not welcome such an intrusion. Probably she didn't even realize that she was making such a disturbance. 'It isn't as if there were anything we could do. There isn't even anything we can say. Is there?'

Kevin considered this in silence for a moment, then his arms fell away from her. The sobbing continued, at a lower pitch, as though consciously muffled now, but still with the wild despair throbbing through it.

'Ah, Christ!' Kevin turned over, back to her, and she could feel him curl up into a foetal ball. She suspected he had his hands over his ears like a child shutting out an unbearable sound.

Fine! Eleanor lay still, staring up into the blackness, listening to the *diminuendo* sobbing, endless, insistent, intrusive—very intrusive.

It seemed as though Bridie was going to intrude into every facet of their life.

4.

Morning brought a semblance of normality, largely because Bridie remained in her room It was impossible to tell whether or not she were awake, and no one seemed anxious to enquire into the question.

Subdued at first, Nicholas obviously forgot the reason for his disquietude as the early morning routine took hold. His voice rose in gleeful clamour, recounting some episode at school.

'That's never true!' Kevin, with a tentative glance ceilingwards, was egging him on.

'It is so! Mickey Concannon says so. Mickey says—'

Life would take on a new beauty, Eleanor had often felt, once Nicholas got through this phase of regarding Mickey Concannon (a perfectly ordinary, rather tedious, little boy two years his senior) as the fount of all wisdom and breathlessly reporting his every juvenile witticism.

'No, I can't believe that.' Kevin raised his voice temptingly, inviting a reply in a louder tone still.

'It's so!' Nicholas rose to the occasion, or rather his voice did. Eleanor winced.

Even Margaret seemed to feel that she ought to add her bit to the general din and began beating on the tray of her high chair with her spoon.

'All right,' Eleanor said. 'Let's tone it down.'

'That's right,' Kevin seconded cravenly. 'You're making enough noise to wake the dead.' He avoided meeting her eyes.

In the abrupt silence, everyone glanced towards the doorway as though expecting to see a silent reproachful figure standing there.

There was no one, of course. There had been no sound whatever upstairs—not this morning.

'How long did it go on last night?' Kevin had been tuned in to her thoughts.

'I don't know. I fell asleep.'

'So did I.' He shook his head.

'What—?' Nicholas began.

'Finish your breakfast,' Kevin cut him off. 'And don't be asking so many questions or you'll be late for school. Hurry up. If you're ready by the time I'm leaving, I'll give you a lift.'

'And Mickey Concannon, too?' Nicholas bargained.

'And Mickey Concannon, too.' Kevin gave an exaggerated sigh. '*If* he's ready.'

'I'll telephone him, so he will be—' Nicholas started to slide away from the table.

'Drink your milk first.' Eleanor blocked his retreat.

Nicholas snatched at his glass of milk and gulped it down while Eleanor was mentally debating whether or not she should make him sit down to finish it. He then dashed to the telephone in the hall and they could hear the sound of frantic dialling.

'I don't really like going off and leaving you like this,' Kevin said. 'You're sure you'll be all right?'

'Why shouldn't I be?' But he didn't mean it that way, of course. It was simply his way of acknowledging that the situation was one of paralysing social awkwardness.

'You have Margaret,' he said, offering her escape. 'You'll have to take her out for an airing and go to the shops and—'

'I'll manage,' she said. Too late to say it was

something he should have thought of earlier. They both should have given more consideration to all the aspects of having Bridie under their roof. For herself, she could enter a plea of ignorance, having met Bridie so few times, so long ago, and in the midst of such intense personal upheaval for both of them. Kevin should have known better—but Kevin was a dedicated optimist with a gift for forgetting the bad about people that amounted to genuïne amnesia. She should have known better to begin with—and it was too late now.

'I'll manage,' she said again. 'Somehow.'

'Mickey Concannon's ready now.' Nicholas skidded back into the kitchen, cap askew, thrusting his arms into his jacket. 'And so am I.'

'All right,' Kevin pushed back his chair, draining his coffee cup. 'Get in the car.'

Nicholas dashed out again, detouring through the living-room to snatch up his satchel of schoolbooks. The front door slammed loudly, a moment later the car door made nearly as much noise.

'I don't see how anyone could sleep through that,' Kevin grumbled.

'Maybe she isn't sleeping,' Eleanor said. 'Maybe she's—' She broke off. '*Lying low*' was an absurd phrase to spring to mind, but it seemed likely that that was what Bridie was doing.

'Probably she's waiting until we've cleared off. She'll come downstairs when the place is a bit emptier.'

If Kevin thought he were being any sort of comfort to her, he could think again. Eleanor raised her head to receive his goodbye peck with an abstracted air. What was she going to *do* with Bridie all day?

'You'll manage,' Kevin said, going off. He, too, slammed the front door behind him.

By midmorning, Eleanor had developed a new set of worries. Was Bridie going to get up at all today?

Ought she to bring breakfast up to her? At least, a cup of tea?

She had done the downstairs housework first, in order not to disturb Bridie, but now her concern was growing. *Could* Bridie still be asleep? Didn't they have to rise terribly early in convents? Was Bridie making up for lost time? Was it possible for anyone accustomed to rising practically at dawn to sleep so much later at the first opportunity?

Was Bridie all right?

Was she lying up there ill? (Had she gone into a catatonic state? Having seen Bridie, she thought that seemed as likely as some physical illness striking her down.) Might she simply be waiting to be called? Or might she have decided to go to ground in her room—like some modern anchorite?

It was with relief bordering on the hysterical that Eleanor finally heard sounds of life from above. Breathing normally again, she occupied herself with making Margaret comfortable until a discreet interval of time had elapsed between the noise of the plumbing and her appearance upstairs. Bridie, she suspected, would be as embarrassed by the more mundane workings of the body as by any of the more exotic (or erotic) possibilities.

The water pipes began to rumble, betraying that a bath was being drawn. It could now be considered proper for a hostess to appear in the vicinity to ascertain that her guest had everything she might require.

Eleanor caught up Margaret and deposited her in her playpen, giving her a rusk to chew on. Furface stalked over and sat down a safe distance beyond the bars. She and the baby regarded each other thoughtfully. Margaret longed to get her fingers into that tempting fur, and Furface wanted to take a nibble of whatever was in Margaret's hand, with a view to appropriating the entire piece if it were to her liking.

The consequent manoeuvres to these ends would keep both of them happily occupied for a long time. Eleanor knew that she could safely leave them to it while she checked on her guest. There were times when Furface was as good as a baby-sitter.

At the top of the stairs, Eleanor paused and looked around. The bathroom door was closed, as was to be expected. However, the door to Bridie's room was also closed. A 'Keep Out' warning? Or just force of habit? Grimacing at the unintended pun, Eleanor moved into Nicholas's room and began restoring what passed for order in that chaos.

By the time she had straightened the other rooms and made the beds there had still been neither sight nor sound of Bridie. She was no longer even sure whether Bridie were in the bathroom or the bedroom.

The lady or the tiger? Eleanor looked from one door to the other, aware that she would prefer facing a tiger to opening a door to reveal Bridie in any sort of undress, in anything less than full street clothing. With any other woman, such a moment would not matter, but she had the distinct feeling that an 'Ooops, sorry' and a merry laugh would not pass the matter off lightly to Bridie.

But Bridie was here to stay. (*How long, O Lord, how long?*) And a precedent had to be establish at some point, if only to make Bridie aware that there was a certain routine to the day and it would be appreciated if she would make an attempt to conform.

Straining her ears in the silence (*had* the house ever been so quiet before Bridie arrived?), she thought she discerned a faint splash from the bathroom. That meant that she could enter the bedroom and make the bed as a subtle hint that Bridie was not expected to retreat back into it. (Just in case that was what she had in mind.)

She tapped lightly on the door and turned the

knob. Even though she had been fairly certain that Bridie was in the bath, she was relieved to find the room empty. Very empty.

For an instant, she stood there frozen in a shock of non-recognition. How could a room in her home, planned to be warm and welcoming, have been turned so quickly into this cold, bare *cell*?

All ornaments had been swept away, all the homey touches that had been lavished upon the room had been undone. Incredulously, Eleanor stepped inside, looking around.

The pictures had been taken from the walls. The flowers—she glanced across automatically—the flowers were in the waste-paper basket. Even the empty vase had been put out of sight. The room had been made as characterless as a hotel room, without any of such an establishment's compensating impersonal comforts. This room was a place of passage, an ante-room to some other place which might exist only in Bridie's mind. It was somehow isolated—no longer bearing any resemblance to the rest of the house. It was also isolating.

That was obviously the way Bridie wanted it. She had even made the bed herself—as a warning-off? Or because—?

Eleanor crossed the room and stooped to check. Just the sheets and one blanket. The thinnest, most threadbare blanket, the one she had been almost ashamed to put on the bed, hiding it between the thick fleecy folds of the other two because it might provide an additional bit of warmth these chill nights.

Where were the two good blankets? Eleanor straightened up with a faint sigh. In the closet, probably, along with the pictures, the mirror, and every other bit of comfort Bridie had rejected.

Sighing again, Eleanor let her hand hover above the back of the *prie-dieu* as she looked around hopelessly. Neither she nor Kevin had ever had any real conviction that Bridie was going to be able to settle down as a member of the family, so why should she feel so despairing at this firm evidence of the fact?

Shaking her head, she turned away. As she did so, her fingers touched and recoiled from something stiff and harsh lying over the back of the *prie-dieu*. The thing slid stiffly to the floor at her feet.

Eleanor looked down incredulously. Automatically, she bent to pick it up, but her fingers recoiled again from the wiry anachronism. She had to force herself to grasp it and lift it. Her mind, too, was recoiling.

These things didn't happen in this day and age. This—this monstrosity couldn't exist.

But it did—and Bridie owned it. Wore it. A hair shirt.

Eleanor dropped it over the back of the *prie-dieu*, no longer able to hold it. Was that the way it had lain there before? If it wasn't, would Bridie notice? Know that someone had entered her room in her absence?

Eleanor had the sudden feeling of being an intruder in her own home. A trespasser. A spy.

She had to get out of this room!

Soundlessly, swiftly, she fled, no longer caring whether the *prie-dieu* might betray her inspection. She closed the door silently behind her and shuddered, instinctively glancing down the hall to make sure the bathroom door was still closed. It was. She had escaped without discovery this time—and there would not be a next time. She would not enter Bridie's room again.

She did not even want to encounter Bridie again. That could not be avoided altogether, but certainly it could be postponed for a while. She found that the impulse towards flight had not left her—she wanted to get out of the house itself now. She needed time to regain her composure before she could face Bridie again without betraying how much unsought-for, unwelcome knowledge she possessed.

At the top of the stairs, she hesitated. She could not leave the house without saying anything to Bridie. She looked back down the hallway and raised her voice reluctantly.

'Bridie? . . . Bridie?'

There was a faint covert sound, as of a movement arrested in midsplash. Bridie was listening.

'Bridie, I—I have to go out for a while. To the shops—and Margaret needs an airing. You—you'll be all right, won't you . . . ?' Her voice faltered; she broke off, listening. To the silence.

'Bridie, did you hear me?' Her voice was stronger; she would not be cheated of her brief escape.

'I must go out. You'll have to get your own breakfast, I'm afraid. Help yourself to anything you want. Anything at all. I'll be back in about two hours.'

'Thank you . . .' Very faintly, from very far away, from a much greater distance than just the bathroom. '. . . very kind . . .' The muted splashing resumed.

Eleanor skimmed down the stairs, fleeing from the sudden certainty that the water in the bath was ice-cold, that no water softener had been used, nor even soap, that Bridie was scrubbing her hated flesh with an uncompromising brush, that the only breakfast Bridie would help herself to—if she ate at all— would be a cup of tea with neither sugar nor milk and a piece of dry toast.

Why did people do such things to themselves? What hatred of life, what terror of after-life possessed them? How much worse could any hypothetical hell be than the hells they inflicted on themselves in this world?

She snatched up Margaret and popped her into her pram, ignoring the semi-gnawed rusk that went flying to the floor to be pounced on by Furface.

Margaret gurgled with delight; such haste was

most unusual, but amusing. She babbled incoherent encouragement as the pram flew down the hallway, which turned to noises of impatience as their progress halted for her mother to open the front door.

'Shhh,' Eleanor said automatically, scarcely knowing why she did so. 'Shh, we'll be out of here in a second now.'

In the sudden silence, while she struggled with the latch, she heard a distant sound. It was a faint dry whooshing sound, then a light soft clatter, repeated over and over again.

For a chilling moment, Eleanor wondered what Bridie was doing now. Then she recognized the noise.

It was the most domestic sound in the world and she had heard it often before. It was Furface. Having discovered that the rusk was unpalatable, Furface was now trying it out as a toy, sending it flying across the linoleum with a flick of her paw and clattering after it to catch it before it stopped moving. Eleanor would have laughed at herself if her disquiet had not shown her how deeply Bridie's presence had begun preying on her nerves.

She manoeuvred the pram through the door and down the step, surprised to find the sun shining. The atmosphere inside the house was such that she had thought it bleak and grey everywhere.

She hesitated, then gave way to temptation and slammed the front door loudly behind her. Bridie might take it as a signal that the house was empty now, but Eleanor felt that in some small way the intrusive noise helped to re-establish her sovereignty over her own domain.

5.

Across the street, a lace curtain twitched. Eleanor lifted her chin, smiled brightly and gave a cheerful wave. The curtain twitched again and no further movement was visible.

Eleanor sighed faintly, but kept smiling as she wheeled the pram down the path in a more measured progress than she had used getting out of the house. It was too much to hope that the neighbours were not going to be interested.

Even now she could feel the eyes boring through the lace curtain. Mickey Concannon's mother was as tedious as her son, and as predictable. Fortunately, she had 'flu—and that prevented her from appearing at the door with a loaf of soda bread and expectant look, waiting to be invited in, to stare around, to pounce on Bridie and inspect her.

And yet, the situation was not new. History repeats itself. Once before, there had been a Dissolution of the Monasteries. Now, because history never repeats itself in exactly the same way, the dissolution was coming from within. That was the difference, the reason, perhaps, for the prurient curiosity of the neighbours. The entire Church structure was changing, and Bridie was the first harbinger of that change in this neighbourhood.

For the first time, Eleanor felt a twinge of sympathy for those families in the past—those unsung heroes and heroines who had been hit by the first Dissolution, who had found themselves with embarrassing relatives suddenly on their doorsteps. Had they, too, been faced with prying, probing neighbours watching their every move? How had they explained away the sudden appearance of an Uncle Dominic— he of the curious tonsure—within the family circle?

Every generation had its problems.

Abandoning the historical perspective, Eleanor turned the pram towards Veronica's house, realizing that she had promised last night to drop in. And realizing also that, if she went there before doing her shopping, she had an excuse to break away with the plea that she still had to visit the shops.

She wondered if Mrs Concannon had heard yet that Dee-Dee was back. If so, she must be bewildered by the richness of choice available to her: Which scandal took precedence? Which house to watch? It was to be hoped that she found time to make Mickey's dinner tonight. (It was to be very much hoped— otherwise she might find Mickey had cadged an invitation from Nicholas and was dining with them.)

An empty pram was already standing beside the back steps as she turned in at the gate. She parked Margaret's beside it with relief—that meant Carmel was here, with Pegeen, her youngest. As she lifted Margaret, she heard a burst of laughter from the kitchen and smiled as she hurried up the steps. The situation must be well under control here if everyone were relaxed enough for merriment. Or perhaps Veronica had slipped something into Mam's tea—as she sometimes darkly threatened to do when her mother was behaving especially unreasonably.

'Come in.' The door swung open at her first tap, and Veronica stood there, looking too harassed to have possibly put Mam beyond the range of making difficulties. It was clear that Veronica had not been joining in the family laughter.

'Ellie, you're late!' Carmel raised her teacup in salute. 'We expected you ages ago. What's kept you—did you have to join in the morning devotions with Bridie?'

'I managed to restrain my enthusiasm,' Eleanor said dryly. 'Hello, Dee-Dee.'

'Eleanor!' Dee-Dee swooped at her and brushed cheeks then settled, quite properly, to cooing over Margaret.

'If you'd like to hold her—' Eleanor offered, trying to shift Margaret into her arms.

'Oh no, no.' Dee-Dee backed away. She was wearing a beautifully tailored suit in a muted blue-green tweed with a blue silk blouse. 'I'll wait till I've had one or two of my own and am used to them. I wouldn't want to drop her, or anything.'

'Have a cup of tea.' Carmel was already pouring it out. 'And tell us how you've been getting on. We've been dying to hear.'

'There isn't really anything to tell.' She could not bring herself to betray Bridie's grim little secret of the hair shirt. 'Bridie hadn't come downstairs when I left, and I want to get to the shops—' She slipped that in quickly, casually depositing Margaret on the floor beside a placidly welcoming Pegeen. 'So I'm afraid I had to go out and leave her to get her own breakfast.' She was assailed by a fresh onslaught of guilt. 'You don't think that was *too* awful of me, do you?'

The burst of laughter was reassuring. To her, at least. But it made Veronica glace upwards apprehensively.

'Mam isn't feeling well.' Veronica did not look towards Dee-Dee. 'She's staying in bed today.'

'Like mother, like daughter,' Carmel said cheerfully.

'Watch your language!' Dee-Dee carefully just missed Carmel's head with a playful cuff.

Veronica moved her head protestingly, frowning, looking as though she would have liked to shush them both. Eleanor felt a rush of sympathy. It was thoughtless, as well as tactless, of those two to make so much noise, and to sound as though they were enjoying themselves. When Mam decided to lie ill, she expected the whole house to revolve around her (even more so than usual) and she would blame Veronica for any defection. Worse, she would find some way of taking it out of Veronica later.

'Sit down, Veronica,' Dee-Dee said impatiently, 'and finish your tea. Don't hover there flapping.'

'Yes,' Veronica said vaguely. 'Yes, I will, in a minute.' She turned pleading eyes on Eleanor. 'Wouldn't you like to go upstairs for a minute and—and say hello to Mam? She'll rest easier knowing who's down here.'

There was nothing Eleanor would have liked less, but she couldn't very well say so. She agreed weakly.

'You, too, Carmel,' Veronica said. 'You haven't been up yet.'

'I've been waiting for Eleanor.' Carmel heaved herself out of her chair. 'I'm not going up there unless I can travel in convoy.'

'Shall I come too?' Dee-Dee challenged Veronica mischievously. 'I haven't seen dear Mam since I've been back.'

'Oh, she isn't well enough for too much excitement,' Veronica said hastily, too anxious to realize she was being teased. 'I'm sure she'll want to see you— later.'

'Oh, Veronica!' Dee-Dee laughed, her eyes hard and bright. 'Do you think I don't know? The only way Mam wants to see me is in my coffin.'

'No, no,' Veronica protested. 'Honestly, Dee-Dee—'

'Honestly, indeed,' Dee-Dee jeered. 'Stop trying to cover for her. *I* know what she's like.'

'She's only upset right now,' Veronica said. 'She'll get over it. She'll really be glad you're here—once she's used to the idea.'

'A likely story!' Dee-Dee shook her head. 'Still trying to protect us all from each other—and still getting caught in the middle, as usual. You're too nice for this family, 'Ron, that's your trouble. You're not tough enough. You should have got out from under years ago—the way the rest of us did.'

'No, Dee-Dee—' Veronica pushed back a straying strand of hair in a distraught motion.

'Come on, Eleanor.' Carmel took her arm and drew her towards the doorway. 'Let's get it over with.'

The curtains were drawn in the bedroom and Mam was a black hulk in the darkness, huddled in the great double bed, with the gleam of her eyes like an animal's shining out of a dark cavern.

'Veronica says you're not feeling well.' Carmel was always able to say something to cover awkward pauses. 'Are you any better now?'

A discontented grumbled answered her.

'That's too bad—' Eleanor tried to weigh in and keep up her end of the conversation to help Carmel. She could not finish the sentence, forgetting what she had been intending to say as the gleaming malevolent eyes transferred their attention to her.

She had never quite been able to cope with Mam's barely-concealed hostility. She found herself resorting to a cool distant politeness, retreating behind anyone else present and making her escape as soon as possible. It was nothing so simple as religious discrimination—Mam did not really like Carmel, either.

Instinctively, she moved closer to Carmel, only to

perceive through the gloom that Carmel appeared to waver and clutch at the foot of the bed for support.

'Carmel, what's the matter?' She put her arm around Carmel, alarmed at the dead weight as Carmel sagged against her.

'What's the matter?' Mam echoed from the bed with sudden animation. 'What's wrong with her?'

'It's nothing,' Carmel said weakly. 'I just came over faint for a minute. I'll be all right.' But she continued to lean heavily on Eleanor.

'Take her downstairs,' Mam ordered sharply. 'I can't have her sick in here.'

'She isn't going to be sick,' Eleanor said evenly, fighting back a surge of anger. It was typical of Mam to worry only about her own comfort, with no thought for poor Carmel. 'And I'm not sure she could manage the stairs right now. Let her sit down for a few minutes.' (By rights, Mam ought to get out of bed and let Carmel lie down. But, face it, it would take someone a lot braver than *she* was to suggest that.)

'Come on.' She tried to urge Carmel towards the armchair by the window. 'Come and sit down. Can you make it?'

'Yes, yes, I think so.' Carmel fell heavily into the chair and closed her eyes.

'It's not the baby coming, is it?' Eleanor worried.

'Get her out of here,' Mam said. 'I'm not having a mess on my good carpet.'

Eleanor opened her mouth to reply rudely, but felt Carmel's hand tighten warningly around her wrist. She looked down and Carmel winked conspiratorially.

'I think I can make it downstairs . . . probably,' Carmel said. 'If I can just lean on you . . . I'll be better off down there . . . if anything . . . happens.'

'Yes, of course,' Eleanor agreed. She helped Carmel out of the chair. If anything happened, it would much better happen on the ground floor, where stretcher-bearers from an ambulance would find it easier to get in and out.

'That's right.' Mam urged them through the door. 'That's right. Get her downstairs. Hurry.'

'I don't think hurrying would be a good idea,' Eleanor said, vaguely conscious of a muffled snort from Carmel. 'We don't want any accidents.'

'*Who* doesn't?' Carmel muttered, *sotto voce*. 'It would suit that one just fine if we both fell downstairs and never got up again.'

'Eleanor—' Mam's call halted them just outside the door. Leaving Carmel propped against the wall, she went back in.

'Yes?'

'You can tell Veronica to bring up my tea now.' There was a clotted satisfaction in Mam's voice. 'I think I could manage some now. I'm feeling a bit brighter.'

Eleanor restrained herself from slamming the door. Of all the selfish— She turned to find Carmel standing up straight and her usual smiling cheerful self again.

'You're all right,' Eleanor said.

'Of course I am. Why shouldn't I be? Oh, that performance in there?' Carmel winked again. 'I just wanted to cheer Mam up. And didn't I just? Made her day, the rotten old cow!'

'Carmel, you're impossible!'

'Impossible? Just because I wanted to make her think she was getting her money's worth?'

'Now really—'

'You don't know, do you?' Carmel surveyed her thoughtfully. 'You're such an innocent.'

'I'm not!' Eleanor was relieved to see that Carmel was descending the long steep staircase without difficulty, although keeping a hand on the railing for balance.

'No? Oh, I suppose it's the way you've been

brought up. You don't believe things like that can happen. Perhaps, in your world, they don't.'

'What things?'

'Mam—and the kind of Church-centered, twisted mind she has.' Carmel paused, looking at Eleanor steadily. 'She's warped all the way through. You know that, don't you?'

'I suppose I do,' Eleanor said uneasily. It was something she would have enjoyed following up in other circumstances. But, standing here on the stairs, with Mam above and two of her daughters below, the conversation made her acutely uncomfortable. At any moment, Veronica or Dee-Dee might come out of the kitchen and hear what they were saying.

'She hates us.' Carmel stated the irrefutable fact. 'You can't have missed that. She'd like to be rid of both of us and have her sons back again—and there's only one way she can think of. She's hoping we'll die in childbirth—especially me.'

'Oh, but—' Eleanor stopped. It seemed all too likely.

'Yes, she is,' Carmel said. 'Why else do you suppose she gives Pat money every time he makes me pregnant? It's a bonus for work well done. Oh—he doesn't realize what's behind it. He won't let himself. But I'm on to her—the old besom—and it won't work. I'm too strong and too healthy. I'll live to dance on her grave and, begod! roll on the day!'

She began descending the stairs again slowly and Eleanor, aghast, followed her.

'You don't know how lucky you are with your Kevin,' Carmel went on. 'He's taking better care of you than you know. Although—'

She halted again, looking up at Eleanor. 'There's quite a coincidence with my Pegeen and your Margaret being so close together. Or did you never think of it?'

'That's absurd,' Eleanor said. 'I *wanted* Margaret.'

'Oh, I believe that,' Carmel assured her. 'I'm just suggesting that, as it was happening anyway, maybe Kevin wasn't above letting Mam think—'

Eleanor remembered the sidelong looks, the sly digs. She had ignored them at the time, serene in the assurance that her child was planned and intended. She thought it couldn't matter if Mam got some sort of obscure satisfaction out of believing she had been 'caught'. And had Mam been so smug and complacent through it all because she believed she had suborned Kevin into forcing another child on his Protestant wife?

'Didn't you ever notice—' Carmel prodded. 'Kevin seemed a bit flush with money at the time. He even bought you a new refrigerator, as I recall.'

Eleanor recalled it, too. She recalled, with hindsight, his odd, almost embarrassed reaction to her delight. (Kevin, sharing his ill-gotten gains, but unable to admit it? Afraid to let her know the deception he had practised?)

'And good luck to him, I say.' Carmel spoke quickly, as though belatedly recognizing the extent of her indiscretion and trying to cover it up. 'Don't look like that, Ellie—the old bag had it coming to her.'

'I'm all right.' Eleanor tried to pull herself together and not let Carmel see how much the news had shaken her. (Carmel was right—they *had* been brought up in two different worlds and, just when she thought she was comfortably at home in this world and understood it, an abyss opened up beneath her feet like a crack in a glacier that had looked solid and safe to venture out on.)

'Did I say you weren't?' Carmel still looked guilty. 'Come on, Ellie, don't take it so seriously. Why should it bother you if Kevin turned a profit on something that was going to happen anyway? Laugh it off—'

'Don't stand out here nattering all day, you two.'

Dee-Dee, laughing, came into the hallway and looked up at them. 'Come and have another cup of—'

A key scraped in the front door and it swung open abruptly. Blinking as he stepped out of the sunlight into the gloom, Terence entered the hall. It was too late for Dee-Dee to escape back into the kitchen, he had already heard her voice. The blind, hopeful twist of her head showed that. He frowned into the darkness, seeking her, and finding her.

'Dee-Dee?' It was indecent, Eleanor thought, that a man should betray himself so completely. She wished she were somewhere else at this moment—anywhere else.

'Terry—' Dee-Dee's voice was cool, guarded. 'I didn't expect— Veronica said you'd be tied up at sales conferences all week.' *Out of the way*— The unspoken thought behind her words was all too clear.

'Did she?' Terence flushed. 'I was—that is, I am. But I needed some papers I'd left in my room. So I came—' He broke off, abandoning formalities, too much showing in his eyes, quivering in his voice, betraying him hopelessly.

'Dee-Dee, you've come back! I'm so glad to see you— I've been waiting—'

Yet another world. Terence's world. A world that did not recognize divorce, a world in which Dee-Dee was still his lawful wedded wife. And he was only too ready to welcome her back to it.

'I'm just here for a few days.' Dee-Dee's face froze, her voice was cold and incisive as a surgeon's knife cutting away dead flesh. (*'And they shall be two in one flesh.'*) 'I've just brought my fiancé up to introduce him to the family.'

'Oh, I see.' Terence's outstretched arms dropped to his side. (*Dead flesh falling away from the wound.*) 'Well . . . well . . . You're looking well, Dee-Dee.'

'And you, Terence.' Cold formality, cold eyes, cold

heart. (To show any warmth now might be fatal.) 'You've been keeping well, I hope?'

'Oh, fine . . . just fine.' His eyes turned away, seeking escape now, but Carmel and Eleanor were on the stairs, blocking his retreat.

'Dee-Dee? I thought I heard—' Veronica came out of the kitchen and stopped dead. 'Oh Lord!'

And that betrayed more than Veronica would ever have wanted them to know. (But how could they have known her for so long and never guessed?)

Eleanor exchanged glances with Carmel and, as one, they moved down the remaining stairs and clear to the staircase, opening a path of escape to Terence, if not to Veronica.

'Come on, you two.' Dee-Dee had not noticed. The relief with which she pounced on Carmel and Eleanor betrayed her own anxiety to escape. 'Your tea's getting cold. What were you *doing* up there? I can't believe Mam's turned into a scintillating conversationalist at this late stage—' She herded them towards the kitchen, past an unseeing Veronica.

'Veronica—' Eleanor touched her elbow, hoping it would release her from her spell. 'Veronica, Mam says she's feeling better. She wants you to bring some tea up to her.'

'Oh, yes.' Veronica turned kitchenwards, blindly obeying the call of duty, grateful perhaps for that duty. 'Yes, I'll get it right away.' She darted past them abruptly.

6.

Because it had taken so much longer than she had planned to break away, the shops had been unusually crowded. She had had to queue in nearly every shop and even Margaret's good nature had been severely tried by all the delays. Margaret was fretting quietly to herself as they turned towards home.

As Eleanor wheeled the pram into their own street, a dark desolate shadow detached itself from the lighter shadows at the base of a streetlamp and came towards them. Nicholas. But what was he doing out after dark? (Even though it was only just after.) And loitering—no other word for it—loitering in the street?

Something twisted in her heart as he came towards them with casual footsteps that could not quite disguise how eager he was to reach them. Eleanor decided that she would not make too much of the fact that he was breaking curfew. Perhaps the fact that he was the only child on the street at this hour had already upset him enough.

'You're late,' he greeted her accusingly. 'You're way, way late. I thought you weren't coming. I was waiting for Daddy, now.'

'We were late getting away from Granmam's, so we were late all along the way.' She looked down at him;

he was still wearing his school clothes. 'Didn't you go home and change at all?'

'I *went* home.' He sounded defensive. 'Look—' He stuck out one foot to display a dilapidated bit of patched leather. 'I changed my shoes.' *What more*, his aggrieved tone seemed to enquire, *could any reasonable human being ask?*

'So you did.' Those disgraceful old shoes, salvaged from the dustbin until she had finally ceased trying to throw them out, had somehow replaced his old security blanket. Eventually they must reach a totally unwearable stage but, for the moment, a separating seam between toe and sole gave barely enough room for growing feet.

'Yes.' He took hold of the crossbar of the pram and swung along beside it, making faces at Margaret, who abandoned her fretting and began to laugh at him.

Eleanor didn't push the subject any farther. There was no need to, really. She had no doubt at all about what—or rather, who—might have upset Nicholas enough to send him out without changing his clothes to loiter on the street corner until reinforcements arrived.

And, apparently, not only Nicholas. A car drew up in front of the house as they approached and Kevin stepped out, beaming a greeting at them.

'I skipped lunch,' he reported, 'worked straight through and then took off a bit early. I thought you might like— I mean I wasn't sure but what the weather might have been a bit heavy—' He glanced down at Nicholas, who was elaborately trying to pretend that he hadn't cracked that particular grown-up code.

'Glory be to God!' He had caught sight of Margaret's face, peeping like some forest animal's through an underbrush of grocery bags. 'Whatever's all that?'

'We're having company tonight,' Eleanor explained.

'A party?' Nicholas asked hopefully.

'I suppose you could say so—' Eleanor met Kevin's eyes. 'Veronica, Carmel and Patrick, Dee-Dee and James—'

'Is Mam coming?' Kevin sounded as wary as Nicholas might.

'I doubt it.' (*Dear God, not that!*) 'Mam—uh—' Now she glanced quickly at Nicholas. 'Mam isn't feeling well. She stayed in bed today.'

'The best thing, I'm sure.' Kevin's heartiness rang hollow. 'Does she—?' The twitch of his eyebrow finished the sentence: *know about Bridie yet?*

'I don't think so.' Eleanor took out her key and inserted it in the lock. 'I think Veronica decided Dee-Dee was enough for her to cope with at the moment.'

'Quite right, quite right.' Kevin took custody of the pram and wrestled it into the front hall. Nicholas, she noticed, had slipped sideways and fallen-in behind them, so that he was at the rear as they approached the kitchen, Eleanor carrying Margaret and Kevin coping with the miscellaneous bags of shopping.

The kitchen seemed unnaturally spotless and empty, with no sign that humans had ever inhabited it. Eleanor put Margaret into the playpen (even that seemed to have been tidied) and looked around uneasily.

Nothing one could put one's finger on, but the certain innate knowledge that someone else's hand had been at work in this her domain, somehow making it less hers. It seemed colder, somehow, barren—as though life had been withdrawn from it by some giant hypodermic needle, leaving a sealed vacuum of empty space.

'Prrr-yeow?' Then Furface eeled out from under the fridge and advanced on her, uttering loud complaints. (The fridge—no, she would think about that later. Much later.)

'What's the matter with Furface?' Kevin watched, puzzled, as the cat marched back and forth between himself and Eleanor, declaiming some long list of feline injustices. 'Something's happened to upset her.'

'I don't know,' Eleanor said thoughtfully. 'She was all right when we left.'

'Come on, old girl.' Kevin stooped and reached for Furface, but she eluded him, still complaining bitterly.

'Have some milk,' Eleanor said placatingly. 'Where's your dish?' They always left a saucer of fresh milk, frequently replenished, beside the stove, so that Furface could help herself when she chose to.

Furface gave her a smouldering glare and lashed her tail indignantly. Obviously, that was part of the problem.

'Someone's been tidying up.' Kevin didn't miss as much as he sometimes seemed to. (Or was it that he had had experience of Bridie of old?)

Eleanor crossed to the sink and stopped, looking down, feeling as though she had received an abrupt slap in the face. The sink was empty, bare, shining. Not the way she had left it. (But she had left it the way she wanted it.) There had been a jam-jar of slightly clouded water in which she was rooting a slip of Carmel's begonia. Also the two halves of a saucer, broken by Nicholas yesterday morning, had been waiting until she had a chance to glue them together. Bridie's arrival last night had interrupted her plans. (Dear God, was it only last night? Was it possible that this interloper had been disrupting her home for less than twenty-four hours?)

'What's the matter?' Kevin crossed to stand beside her. 'Now it's *your* fur that's ruffled. What's she done?'

Eleanor moved to one side and stepped on the

dustbin treadle, the lid flew open and she saw everything—the begonia slip, trailing threads that would never flourish because the stem had been snapped. And the saucer—not just the two pieces she had so carefully tried to preserve, but an assortment of shards and chips looking as though they had been hurled into the bin with unnecessary violence. Or with the smug self-righteousness of one who was correctly performing the actions that were really another's duty. In either case, the favourite saucer was unmendable now.

'Oh-oh.' Kevin gave a low whistle. 'I'm sorry, love.' He patted her shoulder. 'I'll buy you a new one tomorrow.'

'You can't. It's out of stock.' Tight-lipped, Eleanor turned and opened one of the cabinets above the sink. Sure enough, Furface's dish was there at the bottom, shining clean, but segregated from the family dishes. She took it out, set it on the floor, brought a bottle of milk from the fridge and filled the saucer. Furface strolled over and took a few token licks to establish proprietorship, obviously still only slighted mollified.

'I'm sorry,' Kevin said again. He sighed and added, in the tone of a man who hoped to be talked out of a rash idea, 'Perhaps I ought to speak to Bridie.'

'Perhaps you should.' Eleanor was in no mood to let him off lightly. 'She *is* your sister.'

'Well, now—' Kevin seemed to give himself a mental shake to pull himself together and crossed over to inspect the shopping he had dumped on the table. 'What have we here?'

'What?' Nicholas moved to join him, displaying—Eleanor realized—the first animation he had shown since entering the house.

'Crisps.' With the air of a conjurer, Kevin pulled three packets of crisps from a large brown bag. 'And crisps—and cheese biscuits—and peanuts— Oh, it's a feast tonight, my boy!'

'It's a party!' Nicholas's eyes began to shine. He pulled out ice-cream and ran to put it in the freezer compartment of the fridge.

'It's just family,' Eleanor warned. 'It's not going to be wildly exciting—and you're not going to stay up *too* late.'

Margaret caught the mood and gave a chortle of excitement, thumping the abacus of her playpen with a chubby fist.

'I intended to make cakes,' Eleanor said, 'but we got delayed at Veronica's, so I bought some instead—'

'Quite acceptable. And chocolate, too,' Kevin approved. Nicholas carried them in triumph to the pantry. Even Furface seemed to decide that she had complained enough and settled down to her saucer of milk with a steady contented lapping, tail tucked tightly around her.

Then—suddenly and silently—Bridie stood in the doorway. She surveyed them all, an obscure satisfaction glimmering in her eyes before the lids fell to cover her expression. Caught. Red-handed, all of them. Caught in the act: conspirators.

Nicholas backed against the wall, then slid down it as though the bones in his legs had turned to jelly, landing in a forlorn heap on the floor.

Furface abandoned her milk and, ears laid low, went swiftly to Nicholas, climbing into his lap. He held her in his arms, seeming to derive as much comfort from her as he was giving her. Together the two small heads turned, side by side, to stare at the doorway.

Margaret's hand fell away from the abacus, her eyes widened and she fell silent, sensing an atmosphere she could not understand and did not like.

Eleanor knew that she herself had stiffened. Kevin moved to her side, draping an arm around her shoulders, giving her what was meant to be a comforting squeeze. She did not find it particularly comforting, although she found herself disconcertingly grateful for any support at all in the face of Bridie's silent condemnation.

For they were guilty. Guilty of laughter. Guilty of love. Guilty of conspiring to live their lives happily.

'We didn't hear you coming, Bridie,' Kevin said, too heartily. (*Who'll bell the cat?*)

'You were making so much noise,' Bridie murmured. Even hooded, her eyes seemed to convey reproach.

'We're a noisy bunch, it's true,' Kevin said. 'You'll just have to get used to us the way we are, that's all, Bridie.'

'I'm afraid I was away a bit longer than I expected.' Eleanor was guiltily aware that she did not really want to soften the note of challenge in Kevin's attitude.

'Were you?' The flicker of Bridie's eyelids indicated that she had not been missed.

'I left the tea things out for you—' (Better not to mention how everything had been so thoroughly put away.) 'Did you find everything all right?'

'Oh yes. Yes, thank you.' Bridie moved soundlessly into the kitchen. 'It was very nice—'

'You found the breadbox? I wasn't sure whether you liked tea cakes—' (They had not been disturbed.)

'Oh yes, that was all right. I didn't want any. I—I found a nice rusk, instead. It was very nice.'

Eleanor stiffened. A rusk! Gnawed by the baby, chased around the floor by the cat—and Bridie had picked it up and *eaten* it! Eleanor's throat closed up, she swallowed on a convulsive shudder. She could feel Kevin looking down at her questioningly, but refused to meet his gaze. She would have to explain to him later, when they were alone.

No wonder Furface had been so upset. And Nicholas—had he seen Bridie eat it? Or had he a different reason for the blank withdrawn look that had come over his face?

'That's right, Bridie,' Kevin agreed unsuspectingly. 'You just help yourself to anything you want.'

7.

Carmel was the first to arrive. 'I brought the three oldest with me.' She herded them into the kitchen ahead of her. 'Just let them play with Nicholas for an hour or so and have some ice-cream then I'll send them home and they can take over the baby-sitting and Pat can come over for a while.'

Nicholas stepped forward to claim his guests and they disappeared into the front hall and up the stairs. Carmel looked around curiously.

'When do we get graced with the Presence, then? I thought she might be here helping you get things ready.'

'No.' Eleanor smiled faintly. 'Bridie's gone to "make a visit" she called it. I think that means she's gone to church.'

'It does,' Carmel agreed. 'And I'd encourage it, if I were you. The more time she spends in church, the less you'll have to see of her. And, God knows, *that* would be a blessing. With any luck, you might get her to spend most of the day there.'

'Carmel, how are you?' Kevin came up behind them, saving Eleanor from the need to reply. 'Come and sit down.'

'I intend to.' Carmel followed them into the living-room.

'Have a seat.' Kevin indicated the comfortable sofa hospitably.

'Thanks, I'll take this one.' Carmel seated herself in the old-fashioned rocking-chair. 'It's the only one I can get out of easily when I'm like this. One good backward rock and I'm out of it like a stone in a catapult on the forward swing. And, believe me, these days I need all the help I can get.'

'Due soon, isn't it?' Kevin enquired absently. His interest in obstetrical details was minimal at best and Carmel always seemed to be due soon.

'Another two weeks,' Carmel adjusted a cushion at her back, 'give or take a few days.'

'Will you have a drink?' Kevin put more genuine interest into that query.

'I'll wait till the others get here, thanks. No, wait—' she changed her mind. 'I'll have a ginger ale now, then, but don't put anything in it until the others come.'

Upstairs there were growing shrieks of hilarity. Kevin glanced upwards as he passed the stairs. 'Not so noisy up there,' he shouted automatically, forgetting his policy of encouraging uproar to upset Bridie. Or perhaps the policy only held good when Bridie was actually present.

'I'd ask you how it was going,' Carmel said to Eleanor. 'But you're looking ten shades paler than when I last saw you, so maybe it's better we don't go into it right now.'

'Not with the rest of them arriving any minute,' Eleanor agreed. 'But I'm *feeling* ten shades paler, too.'

'Come over for coffee or tea tomorrow morning,' Carmel urged. 'Just the two of us—and the babies. You can tell me all about it then.'

'We'll see.' Eleanor was not too sure that she wanted to tell all, but a sympathetic ear for as much as she decided to impart would be welcome.

Then the cheerful clink of bottles sounded from the kitchen and Carmel sighed contentedly. 'It could be worse, I suppose,' she said. 'At least, Mam's taken to her bed, and that will keep her out of the way for a while. I wonder if Veronica's got up guts enough to tell her about Bridie yet.'

'She's going to have to be told some time.' Eleanor had almost, but not quite, grown accustomed to the Irish ability to ignore and/or delay specific action until long past the time when the necessary action might have helped the situation. Either the *Stitch in time* philosophy had bypassed them completely, or they simply refused to believe in it. Which, considering some of the other things they managed to believe, was rather straining at a gnat.

'Yes, well . . .' Carmel was singularly unworried about it. 'I suppose she'll find out, sooner or later. I don't envy Veronica the scene she'll create, but so long as it isn't me as has to tell her, I'm not bothered.'

'Poor Veronica,' Eleanor said.

'Poor Veronica,' Carmel agreed. 'But sooner her than me.'

The doorbell rang and Eleanor went to answer it, passing Kevin as he brought in a tray of drinks from the kitchen. Veronica, Dee-Dee and an unknown man who must be James, were standing on the front steps.

'My, we're being formal tonight,' Carmel greeted them.

'I've put everyone on their best behaviour,' Dee-Dee said. 'I don't want you frightening James away until I have him well and truly hooked. After I get the ring on my finger, you can all revert to normal—it will be too late for him to run then.'

Dee-Dee's James had flashing white teeth and a somewhat tentative quality to his smile which suggested that he was beginning to realize that there might be more truth spoken in jest than in earnest in the company in which he now found himself. Or perhaps it was just an attack of suitor's nerves—it could not be easy to be thrown into the centre of a large family group, most of whom were bound to disapprove of him on religious grounds alone.

'Er, thank you.' He took the drink Kevin offered and sat on the sofa beside Dee-Dee. She patted his knee in absent reassurance and looked around.

'Where's Bridie?'

'At church,' Eleanor said. 'She ought to be back soon. I told her you were coming over.'

'Praying for strength, no doubt.' Dee-Dee gave a dry laugh. 'It doesn't sound as though she's changed much.'

'I don't think Bridie *can* change,' Veronica said slowly. 'I think that's why she didn't go with the other nuns when they closed the Chapter House. They were going to a less enclosed Order, where most of the restrictions had been eased—'

'And Bridie never was one for doing anything the easy way,' Carmel finished for her. 'Begod, don't we all know that?'

A faint acknowledging sigh swept the room. Eleanor heard herself joining in. At the same moment, James twitched nervously and looked at the doorway. Instantly apprehensive herself, Eleanor turned. (Bridie had a gift for materializing silently in doorways when people were talking about her.)

But it was only Nicholas, his cousins crowding behind him. 'Can we have our ice-cream now?' he wanted to know.

'I should think that would be all right.' Eleanor silently consulted Carmel over their heads and received an imperceptible nod. 'Come along.' She rose and they followed her out into the kitchen.

She was taken by surprise when the doorbell rang, but, motioning Nicholas to take over dishing out the ice-cream, went to answer it. With a sense of *déjà vu*, she saw the figure waiting on the doorstep.

'Oh, Bridie. Did you forget your key?' She was conscious of sudden silence in the living-room.

'No. No, I have it.' Bridie opened her hand to disclose the key she was carrying like a talisman. 'But I couldn't use it—' She lowered her voice firmly, as though positive her explanation would avert Eleanor's censure. 'Not when you were here—it would be presumption.'

Eleanor bit back a sharp retort, aware of the listeners behind the other door. 'Well, come in.' She stepped back and Bridie sidled past her, heading for the stairs.

'The others are in here.' She indicated the living-room. 'Don't you want to join—?'

'Presently.' Bridie darted half-way up the stairs before pausing to look back. 'First I must . . . my hat . . . my hair . . . Presently.' She turned, darted up the remaining stairs and disappeared.

Eleanor was aware of a snort of muffled laughter from the living-room. It decided her against going in there. She returned to the kitchen. There were moments when the children were easier to cope with than the adults in the family.

Nicholas gave her a wary look, but she decided against noticing the size of the proportions of ice-cream which bulged over the edges of the dishes and dripped on to the table. She also tactfully ignored Furface who was disposing of a lump of evidence that had been dropped by the table leg. It was quite likely that their respective digestive systems could manage the occasional overload of ice-cream without undue strain.

Meanwhile, she had her own guests. Concentrating on the essentials, Kevin had neglected the frills. She shook peanuts and crisps into waiting dishes, meeting the hopeful expressions of the children with a warning frown. Neither Carmel nor she would feel like sitting up all night with sick youngsters.

'Hurry up and eat that now.' Carmel came into the kitchen, looking at her watch. 'It's time you were in bed. But—' her voice rose over their protests—'if you go back now, you can get into your pyjamas and watch television until your father and I come home.'

The howl of protest changed to a murmur of reluctant agreement and Carmel winked at Eleanor, acknowledging that the kids would have stayed up watching television anyway in their parents' absence.

'Hurry up now,' Carmel urged. 'Your father wants to come over and have a bit of party himself. He can't come until you go back to look after the other kids, so be fair.'

'Nicholas—' Eleanor helped a good cause along. 'Will you take these in and pass them around, please?'

Nicholas rose slowly, obviously debating the advisability of dragging his heels in order to prolong the departure of his guests against the prospect of promoting himself to co-host of the adult party and possibly gaining an hour or so's respite from his own bedtime.

'Come on.' Carmel moved to stand behind her own three, which minimally speeded up the motion of ice-cream-laden spoons, although they still groaned protests.

'All right.' That seemed to decide Nicholas. He picked up a couple of dishes.

'Hurry up.' Eleanor found herself echoing Carmel. (How could children move so quickly when they wanted to do something, and in such slow-motion when they didn't want to? It was a wonder more of them weren't battered.)

'I'm going.' Nicholas nodded good night to his cousins and left the room, balancing his laden dishes precariously.

'Hurry up!' Carmel concentrated on her own problems. 'I'm going to count up to ten—and if you haven't finished by then, you'll have to leave it. One . . . two . . . three . . .'

'I'm finished! I'm finished!' The eldest shouted triumphantly.

'Nine . . . ten—and that's it!' The last mouthful disappeared. 'Off with you now, and tell your father to bring over my brown cardigan. I'm feeling a bit chilly.'

The children dashed down the hall, heading for the front door, with Carmel following behind them to stand in the doorway and watch them safely across the street. Coming down the hall to return to the living-room, Eleanor heard the quick intake of breath just before Carmel turned to face her.

'I'm sorry,' Carmel began apologizing. 'I don't *think* it was Pat's fault, but I'll kill him anyway as soon as I get him alone.'

'What—?' Eleanor began, but Carmel moved away from the doorway, leaving the entrance free, and Eleanor could see what had upset her.

Terence came into the house with a diffident smile, but a determined tread. Behind him, Pat spread his hands in mute apology and disclaimer of responsibility.

'I don't mean to intrude,' Terence said. 'But Pat told me it would be all right.'

Pat winced as he met Carmel's accusing gaze and began a pantomime of injured innocence. It was clear that he had been taken by surprise and outmanoeuvred before he had had time to concoct a reasonable explanation as to why Terrence ought not to join a party in a house in which he was usually welcomed.

'Of course,' Eleanor said. (What else could she say?) '*Do* go in and join the others. I'll bring you a drink.' She fled back to the kitchen, feeling that she was taking the coward's way out, but unable to watch Dee-Dee's face when Terence entered.

'I'll kill him!' Carmel followed her. 'I promise you, Ellie, I'll kill him for this!'

'I don't suppose Pat could help it,' Eleanor said. 'Terence would probably have come on his own if he hadn't happened to run into Pat.'

'He would, I think,' Carmel agreed. 'He had that look about him. Oh Ellie, isn't it a mess?'

Eleanor splashed Scotch into a glass with a lavish hand, hoping a large enough portion might ease—or blur—the situation. (What a pity it didn't come in some concentrated form, a glass of which might put Terence under the table.)

'Got the drinks?' Kevin hurried into the kitchen, looking a big grim.

'How is it going?' Eleanor asked.

'How do you expect? We're all fairly civilized. Nobody's thrown any punches yet, but you needn't bother about putting ice in the drinks. It's cold enough in there.'

'Bridie ought to be down in a minute,' Carmel said helpfully.

'Oh, fine! That will warm up the party no end!' Kevin snatched up the tray and departed, trailing clouds of Celtic gloom.

'I suppose we ought to go in and join them,' Carmel said, not making a move in that direction.

'I suppose so.' Eleanor found something else to do at the sink.

'Oh, er—' Veronica appeared in the doorway. 'I thought you might be able to use some help. Is there anything I can do?'

'Come in and sit down, you might as well,' Carmel said. 'Shall we put the kettle on?'

'It's a bit early for that.' Eleanor had always deplored the tendency of Irish parties to segregate the sexes for most of the evening. However, the situation in the other room was a prime argument for the custom this evening, she had to admit.

'I suppose it isn't fair to leave Dee-Dee in there all by herself,' Carmel said.

If Dee-Dee *had* been all by herself, it would have been all right. Although they met each other's eyes, smiling at the inaccuracy, Eleanor, and probably Veronica too, felt a pang of guilt. It *wasn't* fair to desert Dee-Dee in this awkward situation.

'Ah, well,' Carmel sighed. There was a perceptible tension in the atmosphere as they nerved themselves to return and take up their social duties.

Veronica took the first reluctant step, as though impelled by a belated realization of an allegiance owed to the sister who was, after all, her houseguest. She stopped, seeming taken aback, as her other sister shot through the doorway.

'Bridie!' Veronica said. 'What's the matter?'

'Oh!' Bridie halted just inside the door and appeared to become aware that she had been in a most unseemly hurry.

'Someone chasing you, Bridie?' Carmel enquired blandly.

'I—I—' Bridie cast her eyes down, her hands plucked at her skirt as though trying to stretch it lower, perhaps around her ankles. 'I looked in the other room but—' her voice hushed. 'There's no one in there. It's full of *men*.'

'You know them—' Carmel was severely practical. 'They're your brothers, half of them. And you know Terence. The only stranger is James—and Dee-Dee is there to keep him on the leash. You're perfectly safe, Bridie.'

'I—I—' Bridie was engulfed by a wave of red, flowing up from her neckline, descending from her sleeve ends.

'The way they're drinking—' Carmel cast an expert eye at the level of the liquor in the bottles—'we're *all* safe tonight, begod!'

'I— But—' Bridie stammered.

'We'll *all* join the others now.' Eleanor rescued her firmly, sweeping the others before her into the hall and herding them relentlessly towards the living-room.

8.

Nicholas gave them a guilty look as they entered, opened his hand and allowed a fistful of crisps to fall back into a dish. He whirled and pressed the dish upon a bewildered James and Dee-Dee, who flashed a conspirational wink at Eleanor as she took a crisp.

Kevin greeted her with an almost audible sigh of relief, small beads of perspiration marked his hair-line, his eyebrows, the boundaries of his darkening cheeks.

'Time for bed, Nicholas,' Eleanor said, taking in the situation which, thankfully, Nicholas was too young to realize.

Terence was staring hungrily at Dee-Dee, who had seated herself so close to James that it would have been impossible to insert a sheet of paper between them. (What price the common concept of heaven as the place where you would be rewarded with what you most desired on earth? Terence's heaven would be hell for Dee-Dee.)

'We were on the point of mounting a search-party for you,' Dee-Dee said, with a light laugh that didn't quite come off.

Kevin gave Eleanor a pleading look and patted the arm of his chair; she walked over to perch on it. Pat got up to let Carmel sit in the rocking-chair and sank to the floor at her feet, closing one hand around her ankle as though claiming some sort of sanctuary.

Veronica and Bridie entered, glanced at and instinctively shied away from the sofa where Dee-Dee and James were sitting so closely together, and found other seats—also, instinctively, as far as possible from Terence.

'Nicholas—' Eleanor said, feeling an insane sense of urgency. 'To bed.'

'I'm going, I'm going.' In slow motion, he placed the bowl of crisps on the table, searched faces hopefully for one which might signal an invitation to remain, sighed heavily and left the room. They heard his dragging footsteps ascending the stairs.

A new ambience seemed to flood the room now that there was no longer a child in it. Something dark and strange moved to fill some unknown vacuum, tightening their nerves, chilling their blood.

Bridie caught her breath audibly. She stared from Veronica to Dee-Dee, from Pat to Kevin to Terence.

'You feel it, too, don't you?' she asked. 'It's just like it was before I— It's just like it was ten years ago!"

The temperature abruptly fell another several degrees. It was clear that somehow Bridie had dropped a monumental brick. But what?

Eleanor and Carmel, odd women out, exchanged questioning glances—and found no answers. James looked over at them helplessly. The room grew chillier yet.

'Well, it doesn't feel like that to *me*.' Carmel tried to lighten the uneasy atmosphere. 'Begod, I wasn't in *this* condition ten years ago!'

'Since you bring it up—' Dee-Dee leaned forward, leaping so eagerly at a change of subject that she risked appalling rudeness. 'Why are you? I mean, I thought this was the twentieth century? Haven't you ever heard of the Pill?'

'It brought me out in a fearful rash.' Carmel was always willing to discuss her condition. 'All lumps and bumps all over me, and the veins in my legs like a relief map of the Scottish Highlands. No, I got out one step ahead of the varicose and thrombosis. The Pill isn't for the likes of me, worse luck—we're the ones who need it most.'

'But if you feel like that,' Dee-Dee said. 'I mean, if you tried the Pill, then why not . . . ?'

'No,' Carmel said. 'I may not believe it, but I haven't enough guts to abandon it entirely. And *They* won't agree to "mechanical means". But I'll tell you one thing.' Her voice hardened. 'I'll never bring my children up to it. They won't go the same way. They'll never call my little Pegeen "Perpetually-Pregnant Pegeen"!'

'But, Carmel—' Dee-Dee was still struggling to understand. 'If you—'

'I'm trapped—the way all of us are trapped. Not believing, not completely able to disbelieve. But things are changing—and I get a vision sometimes of what *might* happen in the future.' Carmel grew dreamy.

'It comes to me every time I'm in labour. I look into the future—and I see it all . . .

'I see the Throne of St Peter, and Himself sitting on it, worrying about nothing better than next Sunday's collection all around the world.

'And I see some of the new Women's Libbers—scientists, they'll be. Have you read how science can already transplant the foetus of one cow into another cow? One who'll carry it to full term and deliver it? "The Host", they call it.

'Well, science has advanced even farther—and The Host needn't be a woman any more. Even a man will do. Any body, so long as it's a warm, living, breathing body.

'But the Church, the Pope, stay as reactionary as they've ever been. "Barefoot in winter, pregnant in summer"—that's the only formula they have for women. Scientific advances mean nothing to them except a threat. They don't see the advancement of knowledge as any part of God's mercy, only as some new kind of work of the devil. They fight and fight to keep everything the same as it always has been.

'So the women, the scientists, plot together and devise a scheme. And then they begin to put it into operation.

'At first, nobody notices He's missing, the others cover it up so well. "'Flu," they say. "Unwell," they say. "Temporarily unable to fulfil his engagements," they say. And growing paler and more nervous with every announcement, waiting for the ransom demand that never comes.

'Then, suddenly, Himself reappears. Weak and in a state of shock, but they can see He's been well-treated—He's fatter than ever.

'And so they have their *Te Deums* and their Thanksgiving Masses, saying all the time that it's for His recovery from illness, while all the time Himself says nothing at all. No statement, not even to his closest who want to know where He's been.

'But the weeks roll by and the densest of them can see something is radically wrong. He still won't talk about where He's been, or His experiences, but they get in all sorts of doctors and specialists, and they begin to get the first inkling of the truth—'

'*Il Papa* is about to become *La Mamma!*' Dee-Dee crowed. 'I love it! You ought to write it out—it would be a best-seller!'

'Sure, when would I ever get the time? No,' Carmel said. 'It's my own private dream and comfort through a confinement. To think of Himself having to go through one, too, and realizing what it's like.'

'And, after He's found out—' Dee-Dee pressed. 'He issues a new Encyclical, allowing contraception of *any* sort—?'

'Allowing it? He makes it compulsory! Ah,' Carmel shook her head sadly, 'but those other old buggers would never allow it. They conspire together and they get the butterfly-net over him. "Ill-health," they say. "Retired," they say. And they elect a new Pope— another Italian, of course. The rest of the world is beginning to get the message.'

'That's why so many Roman Catholics have started roaming,' Dee-Dee agreed.

There was a faint sound of shallow breathing in the room. Eleanor glanced at Bridie nervously, thinking she looked as though she were going into a state of shock.

'So it all comes to nothing,' Dee-Dee mourned, with a sidelong malicious look at Bridie. 'What a pity.'

'Not quite,' Carmel said. 'Of course, they all think it is. They think they've won. They relax. They begin to forget. And then—' a faint dreamy smile curved her lips—'one by one, the entire College of Cardinals begins to disappear . . .'

'I love it!' Dee-Dee gurgled again, as the others whooped with laughter. 'It gives a whole new meaning to the phrase "Vatican roulette"!'

'It's blasphemy! Blasphemers! Transgressors!' Suddenly, Bridie was on her feet, fists clenched and shaking with rage. 'Idolators!' she added, with slightly less logic. 'All of you! It's sinful to even think like that! Sinful!'

'Come off it.' Dee-Dee looked at her coldly. 'You needn't come the saint with us. You're out of uniform now, you know.' She tossed back her head and laughed. 'They've thrown you out! Were you too much for them? I shouldn't be surprised. You were always too much for *us*!'

'Dee-Dee!' Veronica said sharply. She stood abruptly, glancing apologetically towards Eleanor. 'I really think it's time we were going now.'

'All right.' Dee-Dee was still concentrating on Bridie. 'You can't stand the idea of the future. You're the one who'd like to roll the clock back ten years. Why can't you follow your thoughts through to their logical conclusion? There he is.' She gestured towards Terence. 'Take him. He's all yours.'

'He's a married man!' Bridie recoiled. 'He's married to you.'

'The divorce has been final for years. And, in any case, I wouldn't say married—' Dee-Dee did not look at him. 'Let's just call it "opened by mistake"—like a parcel. He's free, you're free, and—' she patted James's knee—'I've got my *real* man now.'

Eleanor caught one glimpse of Terence's stricken face just before Bridie started sobbing and rushed out of the room.

9.

Eleanor awoke with a headache and a bleak disinclination to move. Before she opened her eyes, she could hear the rain splashing heavily against the windows. Both the headache and the bleakness intensified. Rain. And it was a Saturday. Nicholas, home from school, would be housebound. Neither could Margaret be put outside in her playpen. As for Kevin—

She raised herself on an elbow and looked down at him. The muscles of his face twitched protestingly under her scrutiny, as though he felt himself being pulled up from the depths of sleep. He turned his head away and immediate revenge was wreaked upon him for the sudden movement. He groaned.

'Hangover?' she enquired unsympathetically. 'I can't say I'm surprised.'

He groaned again. His eyelids fluttered back reluctantly, his eyes stared upwards unseeingly. 'What—?' It was barely a croak. 'What time is it?'

She looked at her watch and sat bolt upright. 'Good heavens—it's past nine o'clock!'

'Don't jounce the bed,' he pleaded weakly, as she leaped out. 'For God's sake, don't—ooooh.'

'I'll make some coffee.' She flung the promise over her shoulder as she dragged on her robe, hurrying to the door. Where was Nicholas? By this hour, he had usually been awake for some time. On the rare occasions when she overslept (or tried to get some extra sleep), he was accustomed to either walking into the bedroom and awakening her, or else going downstairs and attempting to prepare his own breakfast—with such attendant noise and confusion that the result was the same. But not this morning. Where was he?

She paused in the hallway, listening, but there was no sound to be heard. A streak of white on the carpet, seen out of the corner of her eye, claimed her attention and she moved towards it.

On closer inspection, it turned into a trail of crumbs marking out a pathway from the kitchen, up the stairs, and through the door of Margaret's room. The door was closed. And Margaret, while showing promise of being an exceptionally bright child, was not *that* bright.

'Nicholas?' Eleanor tapped on the door and called softly. 'Nicholas?'

'Shh!' Cautiously, the door opened and Nicholas poked his head out to peer anxiously down the corridor before stepping back to let her in. 'Shh!' he warned again, closing the door softly behind her.

'What's the matter, Nicholas?' But she knew. That wary glance toward Bridie's room had told her. She looked around, fighting almost equal impulses towards tears and towards fury.

Margaret, damp but amiable, was standing up in her crib, rather damper than usual thanks to a plastic mug of milk, of which as much had been spilt as ingested.

Furface was perched on the window-sill, where the endlessly fascinating raindrops rolling down the pane had been claiming her attention.

A bottle of milk and the remains of some of last night's biscuits were on the floor, where Nicholas had obviously been amusing himself with crayons and colouring book during his informal breakfast.

On the surface, it was a peaceful domestic scene. Until you realized that Nicholas had never before been hesitant about staying in the kitchen to eat his breakfast by himself, had never been afraid of whom he might encounter in his own home.

'We decided to have breakfast in bed,' Nicholas said grandly and inaccurately. He made it sound as though he, Margaret and Furface had held a conference and voted on the procedure to follow. Perhaps they had.

'I see,' Eleanor said, seeing (too clearly) Nicholas's anxious foray downstairs for supplies, his rapid retreat to familiar territory. Seeing her children, like survivors in a besieged garrison, huddling in their fortress prepared to outwait the enemy circling beyond the walls. Waiting for the siege to be lifted—or help to arrive.

'Well, go and get dressed.' She lifted Margaret out of the crib and attended to her briskly. 'We're going downstairs now.'

Nicholas got as far as the door in automatic response before hesitating. 'Is *she* going downstairs, too?'

'She'll probably be down later.' Obeying the herd instinct of adults to stand up for each other, Eleanor added, 'She *is* staying here with us, you know. She's our guest.'

'*How* long is she staying?' Nicholas burst out. 'She's been here ages and ages already. When is she going to go?'

'Nicholas!' Eleanor pantomimed shock, suspecting she was not really fooling her son. (*How long, O Lord, how long?* That was what they all wanted to know.)

'What's she staying here for, anyway?' Nicholas swept on, determined not to be crushed. 'She doesn't even like us.'

'She's part of the family,' Eleanor said repressively, evading the issue. 'She's your aunt.'

'She doesn't even like us,' Nicholas repeated, refusing to lose sight of his point. He was too young to have learned the hypocrisy which dictated that kinship was automatically synonymous with love, liking, and all things bright and beautiful.

'Get dressed.' Eleanor found herself unable to insist upon the lie, even in the interests of adult solidarity. Bridie *didn't* like them. (Did she like anyone?) If there had been anywhere else to go, she would undoubtedly have gone there. But she was thrown back upon the family she had renounced (with what inner joy?) for ever, released from the bondage of the vows she had so willingly embraced.

'I *am* getting dressed.' Nicholas put one hand on the doorknob in evidence of good faith. 'Can I go over and play with Mickey Concannon today?'

'May I?' Eleanor corrected automatically.

'May I? Please, may I?'

'Have you been invited?' The question was rhetorical, she knew. Mrs Concannon would swoop on Nicholas as a starving raven on manna from heaven. By the time she had questioned and cross-questioned him, no facet of life in their home would be left unexplored.

'They won't mind,' Nicholas said, more truly than he knew.

'Well . . .' It would be more peaceful to have him out of the way this morning—but at the price of having the Concannon searchlight turned on every corner of their private lives? On Bridie? 'Why don't you go over and play with your cousins instead?'

'Why doesn't Aunt Bridie go and stay with them?' he asked.

'There isn't really enough room,' Eleanor said regretfully.

'If we took some of the kids over here, she could

have their room and they could stay in the one she's been using,' Nicholas pointed out. He grew more practical every day, especially—like all males—where his own comfort was concerned.

'It's an interesting idea,' Eleanor said, 'but I'm afraid it wouldn't work. You might suggest it to your Aunt Carmel, though.' She spared a smile for the thought of Carmel's reaction.

'Would she do it?' Nicholas asked doubtfully, suspecting adult mockery.

'I shouldn't think so for a minute.' She picked up Margaret and started for the door. Although quailing inwardly, she tried to set a good example to Nicholas by stepping out into the hallway without flinching. A quick glance towards Bridie's room reassured her that the door was still forbiddingly closed.

Going downstairs, she was annoyed with herself. It was too much that Bridie should engender this siege mentality in everyone. Bridie, after all, was supposed to be a guest in their house—not some sort of avenging angel. But—avenging what? Laughter? Enjoyment of life?

Eleanor dumped Margaret in her playpen, started the coffee and determined to absent them both from the house as soon as possible. Let Kevin entertain—if such a word could be thought of in conjunction with Bridie—his sister today. With the hangover he already had, he would scarcely notice one more misery.

When the coffee began perking she poured a cup for herself and set the pot on a tray with just a cup and saucer. Kevin would want it black. She brought it upstairs and set it on the bedside table, breaking the news to him that he would be seeing to Bridie this morning.

'Pour it for me, there's a love.' He regarded her bleakly, almost without recognition. Her betrayal seemed to have passed over his head.

'Did you hear me?' She poured for him. 'I said you'd have to see to Bridie this morning. I'm going over for coffee with Carmel and your sisters.' She amended, 'Your other sisters.'

'Aaargh . . .' Kevin had foolishly moved his head as though in a gesture of denial—remembering, too late, the unwisdom of moving at all.

'I'll have to leave in a few minutes.' She guided the cup into his nerveless hand and then to his mouth. 'We've overslept, you know.'

'Aaargh . . .' The effort of sitting up to meet the cup half-way had done more damage than the caffeine could immediately repair. Kevin sank back on the pillow, his eyes closing.

'Do you understand?' Eleanor tried to keep her lips from twitching (those eyes could open again at any moment). Why was someone else's hangover always faintly risible?

'It's all right,' Kevin said faintly. 'I'll be dead before you get back. I'll never have to face Bridie again.'

'That's just wishful thinking,' Eleanor said sternly. 'Tell her she'll have to make fresh coffee, but she'll find bacon and eggs in the fridge—' (A frisson shook her, but she steadied herself. It was no time to confront Kevin with *that*.) 'And she's to help herself. But I doubt if she will—you know *her*.'

'Aaargh . . .' Kevin was subject to enough frissons of his own.

'So you'll probably have to get up and make breakfast for her,' Eleanor continued relentlessly. Adding heartlessly, 'After all, she's *your* sister, you know.'

'Aaaargh . . .' It was Kevin's last word on the subject. On *any* subject.

Fortunately, Nicholas had opted for his cousins. The children had disappeared up to the top floor, where they were racketing about in some unspeakably noisy game. (They *couldn't* be playing cricket with a bowling ball, however much it sounded like it.)

'Glory be to God,' Carmel moaned, passing cinnamon buns, 'why does it always have to rain on Saturdays?'

'Just to make life difficult, I suppose.' Eleanor accepted a cinnamon bun abstractedly, wondering if it had been the best idea in the world to divert Nicholas here. The noise level had been considerably lower when they'd arrived.

'Thank you.' Veronica took a cinnamon bun, but it dropped from her nerveless fingers to the table. 'Oh—' she retrieved it hastily—'sorry.'

'It's the strain,' Carmel diagnosed sagely. 'I can see it's beginning to tell on you.'

'Dee-Dee will be along in a few minutes.' Veronica overlooked the remark. 'She was going to point James in the direction of town first. He wanted to go for a walk.'

'Begod, she'll be lucky if he doesn't just keep on walking, now that he's had a good look at what he's getting into.'

'He *seems* very nice,' Veronica said dubiously. 'If only—'

'There's no point in "iffing",' Carmel said. 'Dee-Dee's a big girl now and it's her life. Nothing any of us can say will make her change her mind. And who's to say she isn't right?'

'The Church—' Veronica began.

'The Church is changing, itself,' Carmel said firmly. 'Begod, haven't we all been watching them tying themselves in knots these past fifteen years and more? They've managed to avoid every main issue of the twentieth century—and all the time screaming how progressive they are with their pisspot little ideas of progress like changing the language of the Mass and decommissioning a few saints.'

'Carmel—' Veronica's face was flushed. 'You can't—'

Eleanor leaned back in her chair and stopped listening. Why did so many Irish conversations inevitably veer off into theology at the slightest opportunity? It was a phenomenon which never ceased to bemuse her.

Not that the present situation could be called slight. She recognized unhappily that, with Dee-Dee and Bridie both home, there were going to be few family conversations in the foreseeable future which *didn't* hinge on theology and the permitted interpretations of it.

'We're boring Eleanor,' Carmel said. 'She isn't one of us, you know, and she probably thinks we're talking a lot of old codswallop. And who's to say *she* isn't right?'

While Eleanor tried to think of a demurrer which wouldn't involve her in an outright lie, Carmel glanced down at her feet.

'Anyway,' she said, 'I see you came over—bag and baggage.'

'What—?' Eleanor followed Carmel's gaze and saw Furface settled at her feet busily grooming her fur. 'Good heavens, I didn't realize she'd followed us. I'll put her out—'

'No—no. Don't bother.' Carmel halted her motion to rise. 'I'd not deny sanctuary to man or beast—not when it's Bridie they're escaping from.'

'Well, I'm sorry—' Veronica was instantly on the defensive, evidently feeling some personal criticism was concealed in Carmel's remark. 'But I *couldn't* have Bridie there with Mam.' She appealed to Eleanor. 'You *do* understand, don't you?'

'Actually,' Eleanor admitted, 'I don't.' It had puzzled her whenever she had had time to think of it—which wasn't often.

Over her head, Carmel and Veronica exchanged significant looks.

'I mean,' Eleanor said carefully, already feeling

that she was heading for deep water, 'why? Mam *must* have heard that vocations have been falling off so desperately that it's no longer economically practical to keep every school and convent open. Just because, through no fault of her own—' (Almost in over her head. *Was* she so certain that Bridie had not somehow brought expulsion upon herself? *Did* the others in the family know more than she knew? Was *that* the reason Bridie was not welcome under her own mother's roof?)

'I mean,' she continued, floundering. 'There's Dee-Dee—who by your own admission is flouting every tenet of your faith—and yet you accept her as your houseguest and you won't take Bridie.' (For an ignoble moment, the thought hovered that there was a time limit to Dee-Dee's visit. Presumably she and James would have to return to their jobs eventually. Whereas Bridie, out of the convent, had nowhere else to go—one could be lumbered with her indefinitely. It was not a cheering thought.)

'It's no good,' Carmel said to Veronica. 'We'll have to tell her. Although how we can explain it, I don't know.'

'Explain what?' Eleanor looked at Carmel suspiciously, then even more suspiciously at Veronica.

'Now see what she's thinking!' Carmel said accusingly, quite as though Veronica had been guilty of some indiscretion. 'No, it's nothing like that at all. It's just—' Carmel stopped, looking to Veronica for help.

'This is hard to explain,' Veronica said. 'You see, although it isn't really a matter of Church teaching—'

'She means you'll never have heard anything about it in those Instructions they gave you before you married Kevin,' Carmel cut in. 'It's nothing but old wives' tales and Irish superstition, that's all it is!'

'Nevertheless,' Veronica said stubbornly, 'Mam *believes* it.'

'Mam *would*!' Carmel snapped.

'Well, she's too old to change now,' Veronica defended. She turned to Eleanor, still on the defensive. 'It will sound silly to you, I expect.'

'It *is* silly!' Carmel said implacably.

Not for the first time, Eleanor had the feeling that, as an outsider in the heart of the family, she was forcing them all to re-examine long-held beliefs. Beliefs which, perhaps, had never been questioned before. When they were forced to look at them through her eyes, they did not like what they saw.

'Oh, well.' Veronica shrugged, abandoning the attempt to reconcile common sense with religion. 'You see, there's always been this . . . superstition.' Reluctantly, she accepted Carmel's word. 'Among the older people, that is.' She was growing unhappier by the moment.

'Well, they believe that the mother of a priest or a nun is especially blessed. They believe— Well, they believe that the mother of a priest or a nun—no matter what her life may have been—they believe she goes straight to heaven when she dies. Do you understand—' Veronica was growing desperate in the face of Eleanor's bewildered incredulity. 'Straight to heaven. The instant she dies. No time in Purgatory at all. Don't you see—?'

'Do you mean—?' Eleanor struggled to encompass the thought processes so alien to her. 'Do you mean *that's* why you can't have Bridie? *That's* why you're trying to hide it from Mam that she's home? *That's* why you can have Dee-Dee—but you can't have Bridie?'

'That's it exactly!' Dee-Dee stood in the doorway. Unnoticed, she had entered silently and had been standing there listening to them—for how long? 'God bless our happy home!' She sauntered into the room.

'You see,' Dee-Dee said. 'It doesn't matter about me. Mam thinks I've gone wrong, and so *I'll* go to hell for all eternity. That doesn't bother dear mother one bit. It's every man for himself. But Bridie now—ah, Bridie. If Bridie has left the convent, then there's Mam's hope of heaven snatched away. *That's* what will drive her mad. *Her* salvation's been lost.

'Is it any wonder the Irish all grow up warped?'

10.

'*All* that's ending now—' Carmel hastened to comfort Eleanor. 'No one really believes it any more—except the old ones. All the younger people know there's no sense—no truth—to it.'

'And that's why the Church is in trouble,' Dee-Dee drawled. 'Oh, they might never have taught it—but they never denied it, either. They connived at it. Except that they can't keep it going any more. If you ask me, that's why vocations are falling off so. Because the parents can't push their children into the Church any more. They've stopped trying because they're no longer convinced they can get a free passage to heaven just by sacrificing a child. They've got to get there on their own.' She laughed. 'Nothing is as simple and straightforward as it used to be.'

'Straightforward!' Eleanor exclaimed weakly. (It made its own kind of sense. When you knew Mam, when you had seen Bridie. But how could people exist surrounded by such nightmare phantasmagorias?)

'But she's got to know some time—' Eleanor clung to the one straw of practicality she could grasp. 'You can't keep it from her for ever that Bridie's home.'

'No-o-o.' Veronica seemed reluctant to admit it. 'I

thought perhaps—' Her eyes met Eleanor's and wavered away. 'Well, I thought perhaps . . . if we could get her and Bridie to the same Mass tomorrow morning. Well, Mam would see her there—and the worst would be over. Mam wouldn't make a scene in church.'

'Oh, wouldn't she?' Carmel chortled. 'Begod, I'm betting it wouldn't stop her for a minute. It might even encourage her,' she added wickedly. 'It will remind her of what she's losing.'

Dee-Dee's laugh was ribald, but Veronica looked distraught.

'I never thought of that.' Veronica seemed on the verge of tears. 'Oh God!' There was no doubt about it. Veronica was close to breaking-point.

'The sooner you get it over with, the better,' Carmel prodded. 'It's not doing your nerves any good to have it hanging over your head like this. Why don't you just face Mam with Bridie tonight?'

'Oh no,' Veronica pleaded. 'Not so soon.'

'Perhaps it might be better—' Eleanor tried to come to the rescue—'to take one thing at a time. Dee-Dee is there now, but after—' (Tactless again! Departing guests must loom too largely in her consciousness at the moment.)

'After I've gone, you mean.' Dee-Dee laughed, not taking offence. 'Yes, you can break it to Mam about Bridie then—but you'll have to be pretty quick about it. I'm coming back, you know.'

'What's this, then?' Carmel asked sharply. Veronica had gone very still.

'I intended to break it gently,' Dee-Dee said. 'But the firm is transferring James up here. So you won't be rid of me, after all—at least, not for long.'

'So that's why you descended on us so suddenly,' Carmel said.

'That's right.' Dee-Dee helped herself to coffee and

a cinnamon bun. 'It was more than just a chance to introduce James to the family—although I intended to do that, too. Monday morning, James and I start flat-hunting.'

'Then you'll be back in the bosom of the family, so to speak, permanently.' Carmel abstractedly poured more coffee all around. 'That *does* make a difference.'

'Yes,' Veronica agreed in a small, distant voice. 'That makes a difference.'

'I'll tell you what.' Briskly, Carmel began organizing. 'We'd better do it tonight. Eleanor, if you'll let Nicholas and Margaret sleep over here tonight, that will take care of baby-sitting. The eldest can look after the lot and you or I can pop over now and again to make sure the house is still standing.'

'But—' Veronica began.

'We can say it's a Welcome Home party.' Carmel overrode any objection Veronica might be planning to make. 'Mam's not to know how long Bridie's been back. If she thinks it's just happened, she won't be so annoyed about having it kept from her.'

'It might be best to get it over,' Eleanor murmured encouragingly to Veronica, sharply aware that a certain amount of self-interest was involved. (Once Mam knew about Bridie, there would be no reason for trying to hide her. Perhaps Bridie might even *want* to move back into her mother's home. But Bridie was so quiet, so professionally diffident, that it was hard to imagine her actually *wanting* anything.)

'Oh, I suppose so.' Veronica gave in with a defeated sigh, looking numb at the prospect ahead.

'James and I will provide the drinks,' Dee-Dee volunteered.

'We still have plenty of crisps and peanuts,' Eleanor said. 'I'll bring them along.'

'I'll make sandwiches,' Carmel said, 'but we won't need many, will we? It will be best if we all eat first.'

'If you *can* eat.' Veronica was shifting back into her harassed expression. '*I* won't be able to eat a thing.'

'Force yourself,' Dee-Dee laughed. 'You're going to need all your strength. It's likely to be a long cold evening.'

Eleanor shuddered, the memory of last night suddenly upon her again. There seemed to have been nothing but long cold evenings since Bridie had descended like a black cloud upon them.

'It might not be so bad,' Carmel said. 'It might even be the best thing to do. A few exposures to Mam and Bridie will be longing for another nice quiet convent to throw herself into. I don't suppose,' she added hopefully, 'you've seen any signs of her shopping around for a new convent, have you?'

'Signs!' Eleanor felt that she would believe anything. Or, rather, she would believe that *they'd* believe anything. Her mind skittered through a series of possibilities—everything from beams of light descending from stars to cartoon-type hands pointing the path to take. 'What sort of signs?'

'Not *that* kind!' Dee-Dee hooted amidst the general laughter.

'I'm sorry.' Her face must have given her away. Eleanor felt it flood with betraying colour now.

'What I meant was—' Carmel grinned. 'What's been in the post for her? Has she had any letters with return addresses of convents? Or have there even been any plain white envelopes with a little black cross on the back? That would show she'd been writing away—making enquiries.'

'She hasn't had any letters at all,' Eleanor said. 'And I don't think she's written any, either.'

'That's a blow,' Dee-Dee said. 'Still, perhaps we might plant the idea in her head. She may have been so upset by her own convent closing that she simply hasn't got round to thinking yet about the others that are still open.'

'Don't worry,' Carmel said. 'Mam will push it for all she's worth. Bridie will hardly know she's out before she's back in again.'

'It isn't funny,' Veronica protested. 'Not really. Not to Bridie.'

'Was anything ever really funny to Bridie?' Dee-Dee asked. 'If she'd ever been able to laugh, perhaps she might not have turned out the way she has.'

'Well, that's not surprising, considering—' Veronica broke off abruptly. Her gaze locked with Dee-Dee's, then, almost guiltily, they both looked away.

Carmel met Eleanor's interrogating look with a shrug. She didn't know, either. Whatever Veronica and Dee-Dee had been referring to was obviously some deep family secret.

'Anyway,' Dee-Dee said, with an air of changing the conversation completely, 'Bridie made the wrong choices all around.' She grimaced. 'Not that I should talk. I hardly made an outstanding choice myself. Not the first time.'

'You mean you should have left him to Bridie?' The words seemed torn from Veronica. They sounded reproachful.

'All right,' Dee-Dee said. 'Bridie can have him now.'

'She can't!' Veronica's face tightened. 'He's a married man. He's married to you.'

'No, he isn't. And *I'm* not married to *him*. It's a good excuse for Bridie, though. If you ask me, Bridie never would have married him in the first place because she couldn't face the facts of life.'

'Bridie knew the facts of life.' Veronica caught hold of the one point in Dee-Dee's statement she could cope with. 'In a family our size, she'd—'

'I don't mean *that*,' Dee-Dee said. Veronica looked taken aback. 'I mean the other. Haven't you ever noticed how many Irish girls who start studying to be doctors have nervous breakdowns and are never good for anything again? It's all part of it. They can't reconcile nature with religion and they've been taught *they're* the ones to blame if they can't.'

'I know what you mean.' Surprisingly, Carmel intervened. 'You mean the bit about the time in the monthly cycle when you're most likely to conceive being fixed so it's also the time when you're most likely to give in. There's even a special name for that time. I've forgotten it now, although, begod, it ought to be me as best remembers it!'

'That's it!' Dee-Dee laughed. 'That's the bit they can't reconcile. That's where it stops seeming like an Act of God and becomes more of a dirty low-down trick of Mother Nature.'

'I've often felt that way myself.' Carmel nodded gloomily.

'I'm surprised at your forgetting the name for it, though,' Dee-Dee said. 'With your brood, I should have thought you've have had it engraved on your heart.'

'Engraved on my heart?' Carmel lifted her eyes heavenwards. 'Begod, I ought to have it tattooed across my—'

'*CARMEL!!*' Veronica was Mam's daughter. There were moments that left no doubt about it—if doubt there ever could be. Her face was flushed, her eyes blazing with outrage now.

'There's James!' Glancing out of the window, Dee-Dee thankfully changed the subject. It was to be noticed that, like the rest of her family, she often did not like what she had started.

'I'd better go and meet him.' Dee-Dee stood, rather hurriedly. 'We'll get our part of the shopping done now and see the rest of you tonight.' She smiled at Veronica. 'I think we'll have lunch in town. It will be easier.'

'Well, it will work out in the end, I suppose,' Carmel said dubiously after Dee-Dee had gone out. 'But it's certainly going to be awkward for a while, having both her and Bridie around.'

11.

'Ah, yes,' Bridie said. 'Ah, yes. Mam.' A faintly smug look of trepidation settled over her features. 'Tonight. Yes.' She raised her eyes briefly and something untoward glittered in their depths in the brief seconds before she lowered her lids demurely again. 'I *was* planning to go to Confession. But probably it would be best if I saw Mam instead.'

'That's what we thought, Bridie.' Kevin's heartiness sounded nearly as forced as it was. 'You've got to get it over with some time.'

'Over with?' Bridie's voice fluttered upwards, although her eyes remained cast obstinately down. 'But I *want* to see Mam again. I *welcome* the opportunity.' Her voice throbbed with some indefinable emotion and Eleanor was uncomfortably reminded of those unpleasant legends of saints who had cheerfully 'embraced' martyrdom. Bridie was too unhealthily intent upon the scene—perhaps humiliations—the evening might produce. It wasn't—

But who had ever suggested that Bridie might be normal, anyway?

'Eat your dinner, Bridie.' Kevin's dry tone implied that the nuances of his sister's behaviour had not entirely escaped him. 'There's a long evening ahead of us.'

'Thank you.' Bridie took up her fork and poked listlessly at a lamb chop, her face rapt and intent upon some inner revelation. 'You're very kind. But I'm not hungry.'

'If it will make you feel any better, Bridie,' Kevin said, with dangerous geniality, 'we can always kick it around the floor a few times first.'

'Kevin!' Eleanor's shocked expostulation coincided with Bridie's swift, betraying intake of breath. Which was even more shocking. Bridie had *enjoyed* the veiled insult. More, had perhaps unconsciously sought it from the moment of her initial action.

Meeting Kevin's eyes, Eleanor realized that the thought had occurred to him at the same instant. They looked away from each other hastily, guiltily. (Somehow, guilt had become—like Bridie—a permanent resident in their home.)

Nicholas stirred restlessly; the actual adult conversation might be over his head, but the atmosphere disturbed him. 'I'm finished,' he said. 'Please may I leave the table?'

'All right.' Eleanor hadn't the heart to insist that he remain. If it were worth it to him to forfeit his dessert, she couldn't blame him. Besides, Carmel would undoubtedly give them all milk and cakes.

'Why don't you go upstairs and get your pyjamas?' she suggested. 'And don't forget your toothbrush. Then you'll be ready for us to drop you off at your Aunt Carmel's on our way.' She would change Margaret into her nightclothes before they left and carry her over all ready for sleep. It would be easier that way.

'Yes.' Nicholas pushed back his chair hastily, as though afraid she might change her mind, and scrambled away from the table. It sounded as though he were taking the stairs two at a time, and Eleanor felt a fleeting envy—she would like to be excused, too. But the hostess was allowed no such prerogative.

'What time ought we to be there?' Kevin seemed to have been following her thoughts—or perhaps he just wanted to get away, too.

'No special time. Whenever we're ready.' She smiled at him, signalling her appreciation of his unspoken thoughts. 'Plenty of time to finish our dinner comfortably.' (She looked away as she said that. Had *any* meal been comfortable since Bridie had arrived?) 'A cup of tea, Bridie? Or would you prefer coffee?'

'Nothing, thank you. I don't want to be a bother to you.' (The irony was that Bridie probably meant it. Possibly she even thought she was being unobtrusive.)

'I don't want anything else, either.' Kevin pushed back his chair with finality. 'Let's get going. You ready, Bridie?'

Bridie stood, her face shuttered now, no expression decipherable. 'Almost.' She started for the stairs. 'I just want to say a last prayer.'

'Too bad it *won't* be the last,' Kevin muttered under his breath as she left the room. 'You ready, Ellie?'

'You go ahead with Bridie,' Eleanor said. 'I'll drop the children off at Carmel's and join you later.'

'Ahead . . . with Bridie?' Kevin looked aghast.

'You can't let her walk in there by herself,' Eleanor said sharply.

'I suppose not,' he admitted.

'I'll be as quick as I can,' Eleanor promised.

But Margaret was fractious about being put into her nightclothes so early, and Nicholas dallied— the more so once Kevin and Bridie were out of the house. (Eleanor felt some sympathy with him over this. It *did* seem as though the house had reverted to being theirs again, with Bridie out of it, and it seemed a shame they couldn't remain in it and enjoy it.)

Carmel, too, dallied and spent far too much time giving last-minute orders which had little chance of being obeyed once she was out of sight.

'It's getting too much for me,' Carmel groaned, as they left the house and crossed the street. 'Nobody ought to have to put up with pregnancy *and* in-law trouble at the same time.'

Bridie was sitting alone. (Which wasn't surprising.) Dee-Dee and James were sitting together quietly in a corner. In another corner, Veronica and Kevin seemed to be having a muted argument.

'Where's Pat?' Carmel looked around the room, but did not raise her voice. Somehow the atmosphere did not encourage anyone to claim the centre of attention.

'Perhaps it's his turn for the Audience,' Eleanor murmured back.

After hovering in the doorway a moment, they moved over to join Veronica and Kevin. The conversation there seemed the simplest to break in on. Too late, Eleanor realized that nothing in the family was simple any more—if it ever had been.

'I think you might have broken it to Mam,' Kevin was saying, with a degree of censure. 'It isn't right to just let her walk down into the situation, like this.'

'It's all right for you to talk,' Veronica snapped. '*You* don't have to live with her!'

'If the idea upsets you, Kevin—' Carmel smiled innocently—'why don't *you* go up and tell Mam yourself? Pat's up there, isn't he? The two of you ought to be able to break the news with a bit of tact. And that would save any repercussions on Veronica.'

'Carmel! Ellie!' Kevin greeted them with a trapped expression, through which he tried to give the impression of laughing off Carmel's attack. 'We've been wondering how much longer you were going to be.'

'Well, we're here now.' Callously, Eleanor withheld the support he was seeking. (After all, it was *his* mother and *his* sister. Why should he expect to get off scot-free and leave poor Veronica to bear the burden alone?) 'So, you can go upstairs with Pat and bring Mam down.'

'Yes,' Kevin agreed bleakly. 'Yes . . . well . . .'

'Go on, then.' Carmel chivvied him mercilessly.

'Yes . . .' His gaze roved the room, seeking help from some other quarter—any other quarter.

Bridie, as usual, was not meeting anyone's eyes. Her folded hands, her downcast gaze effectively isolated her from the others. Was she praying—or just thinking her own thoughts?

'What time is the Grand Entrance?' Dee-Dee moved over to join them, James trailing uneasily in her wake. Like Bridie, he seemed to have preoccupations of his own. (Possibly he was having second thoughts about the whole situation he had let himself in for.)

'We were just discussing that,' Eleanor said. 'The motion has been made and carried that Kevin ought to go upstairs and help.'

'But not carried unanimously, eh?' Dee-Dee laughed at Kevin's reluctant face. 'Perhaps I ought to go.' Her eyes gleamed wickedly. 'I know how to get her moving.'

'Oh no!' Veronica said quickly. 'You'll only make things worse. You know you will.'

James smiled from one to the other uneasily, then his eyes shifted around the room. They fell upon Bridie and he winced visibly and moved them away again quickly. (It could be a kindness to suggest to him that it might not be too late to persuade his company to change their mind about his transfer up here. From the look of him, the suggestion would fall upon fertile ground.)

'Pat can manage it all right by himself.' Kevin gave his brother a vote of confidence that would have been unappreciated if Pat could have heard it.

Carmel snorted and Eleanor felt her loyalty reassert itself. It was all very well for Carmel to jeer, but Pat had done nothing else so far. Kevin had, after all, given shelter to Bridie and that was no light contribution to the family welfare. It was also not, unfortunately, something that could be pointed out in his favour with Bridie sitting across the room listening.

A silence fell, during which everyone seemed to be mentally debating the next shot in the battle. Eleanor sensed that Bridie's presence was holding more tongues than hers. Perhaps it was just as well Bridie was there, otherwise it might evolve into a full-scale family fracas. On the other hand, if it weren't for Bridie, most of the problems they were arguing about wouldn't exist.

Veronica was facing the door and Eleanor saw her eyes suddenly widen and her mouth move soundlessly. Eleanor and Carmel turned in the same instant.

Terence stood in the doorway. He was smiling with a certain amount of unease and something about his manner gave grounds for the suspicion that he had spent some time in a pub along the way. 'Good evening, all,' he said pleasantly.

'What are you doing here?' Veronica's voice rose above the murmured greetings of the others. 'You're supposed to be at the Palace Hotel right now. It's your Annual Dinner.'

'An' while the cat's away . . .' He wove into the room. 'Is that why the rest of you are all here tonight?'

'Terence, go upstairs and get dressed while I ring for a taxi.' Veronica looked frantically at her watch. 'You still have time to make it.'

'I'm not going.' There was a vacant chair beside Bridie and Terence lowered himself into it firmly.

'Terence!' Veronica's glance appealed for help. 'Of course you're going. You know it's important for your career for you to be there. I'll make some coffee and—'

'Not going!' His stubborn insistence halted her on her way to the kitchen.

'But, Terence—' She turned to him, wheedling. 'You know—'

''Sall right.' He gave her a sly smile. 'I've explained. They understand.'

'Understand?' Her face changed.

'I've told them my wife's come back to me.' He nodded his head sagely. 'All men of the world—they understand.'

'Oh, Terence.' The colour had drained from Veronica's face, her voice was forlorn. She backed away from him.

'Jesus, Mary and Joseph!' Carmel muttered. 'Isn't this all we need?'

'All we need . . .' Terence echoed. His unfocused eyes roved beyond them, seeking Dee-Dee. 'Told them my wife was sick. Not herself. I had to take care of her. They understood.'

'Listen!' Dee-Dee advanced on him, fists clenched, speaking between clenched teeth. 'I am *not* your wife. We are divorced. It's over. Finished. Do *you* understand? Divorced!'

'Ah no,' Terence shook his head. 'No such thing. In the eyes of God—'

'Oh, God!' Dee-Dee whirled away, caroming into James. He put his arms around her; she rested her head on his shoulder. 'Someone make him understand!'

'Terence—' Against her better judgment, Eleanor moved forward. (The others all seemed frozen.) 'Terence, the divorce went through a long time ago.

Dee-Dee isn't your wife any longer. She hasn't been for years. You're divorced.'

'No, no.' Terence wagged his head from side to side. 'No such thing as divorce. *You* don't understand.' He regarded her tolerantly. 'Not your fault—brought up in error. Nothing but a stupid Protestant.'

Eleanor caught Kevin's arm as he began to hunch himself belligerently. He glanced at her and the belligerence turned into a rueful shrug. She smiled back at him. She had known what she was getting into when they married. Well, most of it.

'Terence—' She tried again, sensing that Veronica was at the end of her tether. (So was Dee-Dee, but Veronica worried her more. Dee-Dee had James.)

'Terence, no. You must try to understand. You and Dee-Dee were married once, but it's all over now. You don't belong together any more. She's divorced you—'

'It's no use, Ellie,' Carmel said. 'He's as thick as two planks. You'll never get through to him.'

'Never.' Terence picked up the word. 'Never. "Whom God has joined together . . ." None of *you* can understand.' His head sloped towards his chest. '"Death do us part . . ." Nothing else . . . Never . . .'

'Christ!' Dee-Dee flung herself away from James, whose arms had dropped nervelessly to his sides. 'Listen to me, you fool! I—am—not—your—wife. You *have* no wife. You're free. We're both free!'

'She's lapsed.' Terence raised his head and addressed Eleanor confidentially, as though no one else were present. 'Dee-Dee's a lapsed Catholic. But don't worry.' He shook his head earnestly. 'She'll be all right. She won't marry any other man. She can't. She knows that. It would put her into a State of Mortal Sin.'

'Christ!' Dee-Dee turned away, her back rigid. Even James did not quite dare go near her.

'*Death* do us part—' Terence assured the others. 'Nothing else. Down deep, Dee-Dee knows that. Don't worry.' The sly foolish smile slid across his lips again. 'Mam will make her see reason.'

'*Oh?*' The voice from the doorway startled them all. In the midst of the new emergency, they had forgotten the pending one. 'And *what* will Mam do?'

12.

Shrugging and pantomiming helplessness behind her back, Pat followed his mother into the room.

'*What* will Mam do?' Mam stumped into the room, glaring at them. Especially at Dee-Dee, whom she had obviously pinpointed as the logical centre of any disturbance.

'You'll tell her—' Only Terence was undismayed by Mam's appearance, greeting her as a friend and ally. 'Tell her she's *my* wife. She isn't going to marry anyone else. She can't. She's married to *me*.'

'Of course she is.' Mam's gaze softened as it fell on him. 'She knows that.'

'Then make her come to me.' Terence's voice was anguished; 'She's come back this far—make her come the rest of the way!'

'I'll talk to her,' Mam said severely. '*And* I'll make a Novena that she sees the error of her ways.'

James caught Dee-Dee in a firm grip just as she started forward. He seemed also to be considering the wisdom of putting his hand over her mouth as she began to open it. But, before he could do so, the atmosphere changed abruptly.

Mam had been concentrating on Terence, but now, on the periphery of her vision, she seemed to spot the unobtrusive presence beside him. She whirled on it.

'Who's this?' she demanded, although she could not have failed to recognize her own daughter.

'It's Bridie.' Veronica was unable to let the question stand unanswered. 'She's come home.'

'She can't.' Mam flatly denied the evidence of her own eyes. 'She's in a cloistered order. They aren't allowed out.'

'She's been turned out.' Dee-Dee's voice throbbed with barely-suppressed glee as she hurled the news at Mam. 'The Chapter House has been closed. There weren't enough nuns to make running it an economic proposition.'

'Closed? Economic?' The words might have been foreign, so suspiciously did Mam utter them. 'What nonsense is all this, then?'

'It's true,' Veronica said. 'You know how things have been going these days, Mam. There aren't enough vocations, and money is tight. Even the Church has to make economies—'

'Let her speak for herself!' Mam thundered. She glared at Bridie as though, if she projected enough intensity, Bridie might vanish in a puff of smoke. Back to the convent where she belonged, back to the life of abnegation she had chosen. Safely out of everyone's way—off everyone's conscience.

'It's like they say,' Bridie darted a sly upward glance at Mam. 'They've closed the convent.'

'They never!' Mam backed away, nonplussed.

'They're doing it all the time now,' Dee-Dee said. She laughed abruptly. 'The old order changeth—'

'Nothing changeth—changes—' Terence lurched to his feet. It had been a mistake to draw his attention back to her. For a moment, he had been totally absorbed in the drama between Mam and Bridie, now his own personal drama was in the ascendant again. 'You're still my wife.'

'For God's sake, Terry, sit down and shut up!' Pat ordered. 'This is nothing to do with you.'

'Everything to do with me—' Terence was aggrieved. 'My own wife. Have my rights—'

'Sit down!' Mam gave him an abrupt push which knocked him back into his chair, too surprised to argue farther. He was accustomed, as a paying lodger, to being treated as an honoured guest, figurehead man of the house. Being suddenly treated so much like one of the children unnerved him. He drew back into himself and watched Mam warily.

But she had already forgotten him. 'What are you going to do then?' she demanded of Bridie.

'I'm praying,' Bridie murmured. 'For guidance.'

'Guidance!' Mam sniffed, her eyes narrowed. 'How long have you been back?'

'Just a few days.' Bridie did not look up at her inquisitor, had not looked up since that first darting glance.

'A few days! And they've all been keeping it from me!'

'You weren't feeling well, Mam.' Veronica, as always, dashed in where even St Jude would have hesitated. 'We thought—'

'You thought of yourselves!' Mam snapped. 'You always think of yourselves. Not one of you ever thinks of me, or worries about me. Oh no! I'm just your mother—why should you care about me? I'm nothing!'

'Now, Mam—' Veronica began, only succeeding in unleashing another tirade from Mam.

'Damn the old cow!' Carmel muttered under her breath to Eleanor. 'Just look at poor Pat's face—he'll have another of his migraines for the next three days now, you just wait and see. Oh, I'll dance on her grave! I swear I'll live to dance on her grave yet—the old besom!'

Pat had gone greyish-white—and Kevin's colour wasn't altogether healthy, either. Veronica had visibly shrunk and withered, abruptly projecting a vision of

herself twenty years hence, a desolate creature who
might become an object of pity—or terror, depending
on the way the privation of the years pushed her.
Bridie seemed to tremble before the onslaught—of
course, it had been many years since she had received
the full force of such a performance—perhaps she
was weakened by the decade of silence and serenity
provided by her cloistered walls.

Of all Mam's children, only Dee-Dee, buttressed by
James's arms, appeared able to withstand the gusting
fury. Dee-Dee's decade of respite had been in a
sharper, colder world, where the hurricane gales of
hysteria could herald actual loss of finance or status,
rather than merely the disapproval of a self-centred
old familial tyrant.

Dee-Dee murmured something to James, who
looked stricken and tightened his grip on her like a
man clinging to a life-raft in mountainous seas. She
murmured again and James's arms began to slide
away, while his mouth worked soundlessly, rehearsing
words he might utter if he could summon up a voice.

'And where have you been?' Mam was having no
such trouble. 'Who's been harbouring you all this
while?'

'I've been staying with Kevin,' Bridie confessed in a
barely audible whisper. 'Kevin . . . and Eleanor.'

'Eleanor!' Mam turned slowly to glare at Eleanor,
justified suspicion in every lineament, 'Eleanor!'

The name had always rankled with Mam. Every
time Mam looked at her, Eleanor had been made to
feel that she carried shadows of the Aquitaine massed
behind her, invisible to all but Mam.

A name, Mam had often pointed out, ought to be
the name of a *decent* Saint—like Kevin.

Early on, Mam had related the saga (possibly
apocryphal) of St Kevin to Eleanor with a relish
Eleanor could only feel was sadly misplaced. St Kevin,
it seemed, had been one of those peculiarly Irish

receptacles of sanctity who had betaken himself up a mountain to spend his days fasting and praising God. He was thus minding his own business when a colleen who had had the misfortune to fall in love with him and the utter lack of wit to attempt to do something about it, had climbed the mountain and—

'And *importuned* him,' Mam had intoned, fixing Eleanor with a baleful glare that left her in no doubt as to her mother-in-law's views of her own activities.

But *Saint* Kevin had manfully resisted temptation, wrestling with the devil—and the colleen in question. Unfortunately, in his zeal, he had pushed her off the mountain and she had fallen to her death. (A richly deserved fate, Mam had no doubt.)

Of course, he had to repent the killing of a fellow human being. (Although, Mam intimated, he was fully within his rights and it was a pity other men hadn't the strength to act with such conviction.) And the tears he shed for the rest of his life in bitter repentance and the monastery he founded were the reasons cited by the Church for elevating him to sainthood. (An attitude Mam felt deplorably wishy-washy on the Church's part, when any decent-minded mother knew why the man had *really* been a saint.)

And so, naturally, she had paid tribute by naming one of her sons Kevin.

It had taken Eleanor quite a while to recover from Mam's revelations. It said something, she felt, about a Church which would allot sainthood to such a man. (And perhaps it said even more about a woman who would give such a name to her son—and then boast about it.)

'Eleanor,' Mam said again, bringing the full force of her personality to bear upon her daughter-in-law. 'And Kevin.'

'Well, she had to stay somewhere,' Kevin defended nervously. 'There's no room at Pat's—'

'Eleanor and Kevin,' Mam said again, on a long

sighing exhalation. 'The two of you against me. My own son.' (She left little doubt that he had always been a disappointment to her from the moment he had yielded to his temptress rather than hurling her from the nearest cliff-top.)

'Oh, for God's sake, Mam!' Dee-Dee snapped.

'*You* dare to speak of God?' Mam abruptly switched her fury from Eleanor and Kevin to Dee-Dee. 'I wonder the very uttering of His name doesn't choke you!'

'That's right, I forgot.' Dee-Dee laughed harshly. '*You're* the only one with a direct pipeline to Him, aren't you?'

'Would anyone—?' James stepped forward with a faint air of desperation, perhaps to draw the fire from his beloved, or perhaps in obedience to her earlier muted urging. 'Would anyone like a drink?' He gestured to the bar which had been set up on a table by the window.

Kevin and Pat stampeded towards him as though the words had released them from paralysis. James, acting as quasi-host, poured their drinks with a generous abandon that boded ill for their heads in the morning. Out of the corner of his eye, however, he kept a wary watch on Mam who had given no indication that she had even heard him, far less of being deflected from her target.

'I don't mind if I do.' Terence, at least, had heard and attempted to struggle to his feet.

'You've had enough!' Mam pushed him again. He fell back into his chair, the expression on his face conveying that he was beginning to feel that there was such a thing as being treated *too* much like one of the family.

Dee-Dee laughed again, the light of battle in her eyes. Eleanor began to edge away, conscious that Carmel was doing the same. If it was going to be a family fight, it behoved those who counted as only peripheral members of the family to get out of the way and leave the genuine combatants a clear field.

'Gin and tonic, thanks,' Eleanor murmured to James, who was nervously attempting his bar-tending duties whilst most of his attention remained centred on Dee-Dee.

'I'll have the same,' Carmel said, 'though I shouldn't. Not that it will make much difference at this stage.'

'Yes.' Abstractedly, James poured the drinks and handed them round. 'Wouldn't the others—' he made the suggestion tentatively—'like drinks, too?'

'Don't worry about *them*,' Carmel said. 'Fighting is meat and drink to them.'

'Oh!' James flinched, his eyes returning to Dee-Dee uneasily. The argument at the other end of the room had decreased in audibility but was raging unabated.

'You'll burn in hell!' Mam's voice rose triumphantly, giving the Irish *coup de grâce*.

'If heaven is going to be full of people like you,' Dee-Dee retorted, 'who'd *want* to go there?'

'Please!' Veronica tried to intervene faintly. 'Oh, please! Neither of you mean—'

Terence took advantage of the diversion to slide from his seat and make his way to the bar. 'Don't mind if I do drink with you, ol' man,' he informed James graciously. 'Not your fault. You don't understand these things. No hard feelings. I'll share drinks with you—but I won't share my wife with you.'

For a moment, Eleanor thought James might hit him, but although the temptation flickered across his face, James sketched a pained smile and poured Terence a drink instead. As Terence took it and remained standing there, he poured an even larger one for himself.

'Terence, leave the man alone,' Pat ordered.

'I'll leave him alone,' Terence said. 'I'm not doing

anything. But he's got to leave me alone. Leave my wife alone.'

'Terence, she's not your wife.' This time, Carmel tried her luck at getting through to him, although it was patently hopeless. Sober, Terence had appeared to accept the situation; drunk, he was determinedly obtuse and, worse, argumentative.

'You don't know what you're talking about.' Dismissively, he turned his back on Carmel, on all of them, and concentrated his attention on Dee-Dee at the other end of the room. 'Aaagh,' he shook his head admiringly. 'She always did have the devil's own temper.'

Dee-Dee's temper was closely matched by Mam's, Eleanor thought, watching them. Bridie was giving her usual impersonation of a sanctimonious statue. (Although, was there perhaps a slight feeling of dissatisfaction at not being so completely the centre of attention as she had envisaged?) Only Veronica, who appeared to have given up on her peacemaking efforts, seemed upset to the point of tears.

Reluctantly, Eleanor moved forward. (*Someone* had to go to Veronica's aid—and it was obvious that her brothers weren't going to mix in the situation if they could avoid it.) Behind her, she was aware that Carmel had made a half-hearted move to follow her, but had changed her mind.

'I'm not going to keep arguing.' Dee-Dee's vehemence rather blunted her statement. 'Especially about a world that exists only in your imagination. You don't know for sure, and I don't know for sure. Why can't we let it go at that?'

'Speak for yourself,' Mam snarled. 'There's only One True Faith. *I* know for certain sure.'

'You and all the other stupid sods throwing bombs and bullets at each other over something they've never seen and which can't be scientifically proved to exist!'

'Science!' Mam was pale with fury. 'They don't know everything!'

'Neither does the Church!' Dee-Dee laughed abruptly. '*They* haven't even got their Crucifixes right, it turns out now. Archaeologists uncovered a real one recently and it wasn't the sort you see in Church at all.' She laughed again. 'Now, what are they going to do? Spend a fortune changing all the Crucifixes and Stations of the Cross? Or just try to ignore the whole thing and hope not too many of the Faithful have read the reports?'

'Oh, you can jeer,' Mam said. 'But you needn't think you're so smart!'

'None of us are smart enough,' Dee-Dee said. 'That's been the trouble. But we're better educated now, better fed, better housed, and we've got more knowledge of how to go about finding things out. It's going to be very interesting over the next few decades as religious mythology collides with the results of Israeli excavations.'

'The Church has been going for two thousand years—' Mam spoke with the air of one slamming down a trump card. 'It will go on for ever.'

'Will it? The Egyptian religion lasted five thousand years—but who's building pyramids today?'

'Ah-ha,' Mam countered. 'But that was before the birth of the True God.'

'But, don't you see? *They* thought *their* gods were the True Gods.' Dee-Dee shook her head sadly. 'No, you don't understand. You never did understand anything.'

'I understand more than you do!'

'No.' Dee-Dee shook her head again. 'You've been programmed by a man's religion for a man's world. Whenever there's been any question of divorce or annulment, the Church has delayed and temporized— and hoped the woman would die and get out of their way. When there was any difficulty in childbirth, the

Church taught that you should save the baby's life—at the cost of the mother's. For two thousand years, the Catholic Church has said, "Let the woman die." Now women are better educated than they ever have been before, and we can provide for ourselves and aren't afraid to face our own consciences and make our own decisions. These days, the women are answering, "Let the Church die!" '

'Blasphemy!' Bridie whispered, as though to herself, but loud enough to be heard throughout the room. 'That's blasphemy.' She raised a white, shocked face. 'Blasphemers die. *You* ought to die!'

'Thank you, Bridie.' Dee-Dee swept her with a contemptuous glance. 'I can see you haven't changed a bit.'

13.

'Can't I offer any of you ladies a drink?' James's faint bleat of sanity seemed to release Eleanor from the spell which had caught and held her frozen.

'You can bring me a double,' Dee-Dee called to James. 'I don't care what—as long as it's a double.'

Mam snorted something under her breath—it might have been in Gaelic—and Bridie lowered her eyes again, a dissatisfied frown still rumpling her forehead.

'And Bridie will have the same,' Dee-Dee said. 'After all, she's back in the wicked world now, and it's time she realized it. In fact, it's time we all celebrated it properly. A coming-out party for Bridie.'

Unconscious of the sarcasm involved—or, perhaps wisely, choosing to ignore it—James hurried forward with the requested drinks. Dee-Dee took them and thrust one at Bridie.

'Drink up,' she ordered. 'It will do you good.'

Submissively, Bridie took her drink and sipped at it.

'Can't I get something for you?' James asked Mam, almost pleadingly.

'I suppose I ought,' Mam grudged. 'Something to help keep the old heart pumping. These ones will be the death of me, else.' The look she gave James left him in no doubt that he was one of those pushing her towards an early grave.

'Yes, fine,' James said vaguely, escaping back to the bar with alacrity.

Poor James. This was obviously not his idea of a party. Nor, for that matter, was it hers, Eleanor admitted to herself. But that was beside the point. Veronica had been the object of this intended rescue mission.

'Come on.' Eleanor took Veronica by the elbow, gently urging her away from the others. 'Come and have something yourself. You look at though you could do with it.'

'Oh God.' Veronica looked beaten. 'This was a mistake. Every time Mam and Dee-Dee got together, the fur always *did* fly. I should have known it would be worse than ever now.'

'Well—' Eleanor tried to be cheering—'at least, the rest of it hasn't been as bad as you feared. She seems to have taken Bridie quite calmly.'

'Don't you believe it!' Carmel was beside them, adding her own note of cheer. 'Mam's just lying low. You know how she is. She ignores a situation until she's figured out her best plan of attack—and then she moves in for the kill!'

'Oh God,' Veronica sighed again. 'I wish I were dead! I wish everyone were dead!'

'That's more like it,' Carmel said. 'Spread it around.'

'Here—' Now that she was safely removed from the immediate scene of battle, Kevin was prepared to come to his sister's comfort, if not aid. He moved towards her with a drink. 'Have this.'

Veronica sighed once more and took the proffered glass, looking at it without enthusiasm. 'Drink doesn't solve anything,' she said.

'Perhaps not,' Kevin said. 'But it helps . . . a bit.'

'Does it?' Veronica asked disbelievingly. She took a

sip and stood staring moodily into space. At least she no longer looked quite so near the breaking-point.

'God—families!' Dee-Dee came up behind them, heading for James. 'I'm sorry, darling. I didn't think it was going to be *this* rough.'

'Quite all right,' James said bleakly. He looked at her and his face softened. 'Worth it, you know . . . eventually.'

'God—I hope so!' She slid her hand under his arm. 'I'll make it up to you. Anyway, I'll try.'

'Fine.' Automatically, his arm went round her waist. Smiling at each other, they were momentarily oblivious of everyone else.

'Pardon me,' Terence said. 'But I'll thank you to unhand my wife!'

'Oh Christ!' Dee-Dee said. 'Haven't you passed out yet?'

'I love you, too.' Terence bobbed an awkward bow and his mask of would-be irony slipped away and was lost. 'Always loved you,' he said, straightening up. 'Only you. Now you're back. Here, where you belong. Don't torment me any more, Dee-Dee—' He lurched towards her.

'Just a moment, old chap.' James moved between them. 'She's going to marry *me*, you know. You really must try to realize that.'

'She's never any such thing!' Terence drew himself up with precarious dignity. 'She's my wife.'

'Terence, why don't you go upstairs and have a bit of a lie-down?' Carmel suggested. At the same moment, Veronica moved forward.

'Terence, you *ought* to be at your Annual Dinner. You've still time to make it.'

'Not in that condition, he hasn't,' Kevin said. 'Carmel's right. Go and lie down, Terence.'

'You're against me, too.' Terence drew back. 'I might have known you would be. You married to nothing but a dirty Protestant. You're no better than she is!'

'What?' Kevin started forward, but Eleanor caught his arm. Another phenomenon that never ceased to amaze her was the way the Irish could switch from camaraderie to theology to pugnaciousness with scarcely a pause for breath and with no seeming awareness of any discrepancy in their actions.

'Steady on, old chap.' James made the mistake of catching Terence's arm. Terence wheeled on him in fury.

'Keep your hands to yourself!' Terence snarled. 'If you know how, that is. I don't want them on my wife—and I sure as God don't want them on me!'

'Terence, let me make you some black coffee,' Veronica said earnestly.

'And you're another one, Veronica.' He turned suddenly mournful eyes on her. 'I thought you were on my side.'

'I am, Terence. I just—'

'What's the matter here?' Scenting blood, Mam had joined them.

'Nothing, Mam,' Veronica said, a note of desperation in her voice. 'Everything's all right.'

'You're lying!' Mam said triumphantly. 'You should never try to lie to your mother—I can read you like a book. What's upsetting you all?'

'Go and sit down, Mam,' Kevin said firmly. 'Nothing's upsetting us, nothing's happening. Everything is under control.'

Dee-Dee laughed shortly. 'As under control as it ever was,' she amended.

'*You're* not under control,' Terence accused. 'You never were. And you ought to be. *My* control—you're *my* wife.'

'That's right, Terence,' Mam goaded. 'Assert yourself. Demand your rights.'

'Please, Mam,' Veronica said. 'Keep out of this.'

'Out of it?' Mam swung on her indignantly. 'And isn't it my own house, and my own daughter—and my own dear Terence? Who has a better—?'

'*My* wife—' Terence insisted stubbornly. He made another grab at Dee-Dee, but she evaded him.

'Listen, you raving Irish maniac,' she said. 'I am *not* your wife. I made a mistake—and I paid and I paid and I paid. But the account is closed now. We're divorced. Can't you understand that? It's all over and I'm going to marry James.'

'Never over—' Terence said. 'No such thing as divorce. "Whom God hath joined together, no man put asunder . . ." Nothing personal, ol' chap,' he assured James. 'But it's just not on.'

'Oh, for God's sake!' Dee-Dee exploded.

'Oooh!' The swift intake of breath was the first indication they had that Bridie had crept up behind them. (Did she never move normally? Wasn't she *able* to make any noise? Eleanor began to feel irrationally that there was something uncanny about Bridie's silence. Like the people who cast no shadows, who threw no reflections into mirrors. What was there about her that allowed her to move in such a vacuum of silence? What vow had she taken—what natural law had she transgressed?)

'I am going to marry James,' Dee-Dee repeated slowly. 'Get that through your thick Irish head. I am going to stand up before a minister in *his* Church and promise —'

'You'd be just shameless enough to,' Mam said severely. 'You never had an ounce of decency in you.'

'Perhaps a Registry Office,' James temporized, obviously thinking he was pouring oil on troubled waters. It exploded in his face.

'Worse and worse!' Mam snapped. 'Isn't she good enough for your church? You see—' She nodded to Dee-Dee triumphantly. '*He* isn't going to take his vows in front of his own preacher. That lets you know where *you* stand—if you've got the wit to see it, which I doubt.'

'I didn't mean anything of the sort.' James turned to Dee-Dee anxiously. 'I certainly never meant to imply—'

'It's all right, James,' Dee-Dee said. 'She does the same to everyone. She can twist anything you say against you. She's always done it.'

'And that's all the gratitude I get for bearing you and raising you!'

'And nagging us, and misinforming us about life, and warping us until it's a wonder any of us were ever able to function at all.'

'You shouldn't talk to Mam like that,' Bridie reproved.

'No, you never talked back to her, did you? And look where it got you. Look where it got all of us! We were just damned lucky that—'

'Have another drink, Dee-Dee.' Kevin moved forward as if pushed from behind, Pat at his shoulder.

'Some crisps—' Pat held out a bowl of them.

'The past is over,' Veronica said, at the same moment.

'Is it?' Dee-Dee laughed shortly. 'Then will someone please try to convince Terence of that.'

'Nothing's over,' Terence said. 'Never over.'

'Oh, for God's sake, I've started him off again!' Dee-Dee shook her head in exasperation.

'What did you expect?' Veronica asked.

'You're my wife,' Terence insisted. 'Always my wife—and a wife can't—'

'Don't worry,' Dee-Dee snapped. 'I won't testify against you!'

'I was going to say—' Terence drew himself up, still with that precarious dignity—'a wife can't marry another man. 'S bigamy.'

'*Not* when you're divorced—' Dee-Dee broke off. 'Oh, why doesn't someone take him away?'

'Come on, Terence,' Kevin tried again. 'That's enough now. You're not fit. Let's go upstairs—'

'No.' Terence shook off the restraining hand. 'I'll only go upstairs with Dee-Dee. Nobody else.' He reached out for her. 'Come upstairs, Dee-Dee. Come upstairs with me.'

'Oh no!' Dee-Dee backed away. 'Any time I go upstairs it won't be with you.' She appealed desperately to her brothers. 'Get him out of here!'

'Here, Terence—' Pat had appropriated a bottle of Scotch, and he waggled it enticingly just out of reach. 'Suppose we go upstairs and have another little drink. Dee-Dee can come up later. Let Mam talk to her for a bit, why don't you?'

''S right.' After a moment's consideration, Terence fell in with the idea. 'Let Mam talk to her. Mam will talk her round.'

'That's right.' Kevin moved up on the other side of him. Together he and Pat manoeuvred Terence out of the room.

'Thank heaven for that.' Dee-Dee laughed shakily. 'I don't think I could have stood much more.'

'He's your husband,' Mam censured. 'Your place is by his side.'

'Now don't *you* start again!' Dee-Dee flared.

'I think I'd like to sit down,' Carmel said abruptly. She didn't look too well.

'It's not the baby, is it?' Eleanor was at her side instantly, helping her to a chair.

'Not yet, I don't think.' Carmel lowered herself into the chair carefully. 'But, begod, my condition is getting too delicate to be able to take too much fighting—not even as an onlooker.'

'Are you all right?' Mam called over hopefully.

Carmel groaned encouragingly. Carmel had her eyes closed, but Eleanor was able to see Mam's face brighten, as though she foresaw some good to be salvaged from the evening.

'Don't *you* want to go upstairs and lie down for a bit?' Mam suggested.

'Not *those* breakneck stairs!' Carmel refused hastily. 'It will be easier just to cross the street to my own house than to face those stairs. Pat can help me when he gets back.'

There were faint skirmishing sounds from overhead. Evidently Terence, having gained his room, was having second thoughts about it and requiring some persuasion not to come back downstairs and rejoin the party.

Party! Eleanor suppressed a shudder. When Carmel and Pat left, she resolved, she and Kevin would also take their departure. She couldn't imagine that anyone would urge them to stay on and not break up the party. The sooner this party was broken up, the better.

'Is she going to be all right?' Bridie had crept up on them and was regarding Carmel apprehensively. 'Is there anything we ought to do?'

'She'll be all right,' Eleanor said, as Carmel disdained to answer or even to open her eyes. (But her colour was better and her breathing easier.)

'Shall I make a pot of tea?' Veronica suggested, sounding as though she would be glad of an excuse to escape to the kitchen.

'I don't want anything,' Carmel said, eyes still closed. 'Just leave me be for a few minutes.'

'Perhaps it would be best,' Eleanor seconded her. 'There's really nothing any of us can do.'

Bridie still showed signs of wishing to hover, and perhaps ask more questions. Eleanor moved away firmly and Bridie had to follow her lead. Veronica dithered a moment, then moved after them.

Mam hadn't moved. Still standing at the bar, glaring impartially at Dee-Dee and James (who was beginning to show signs of strain), she turned her head to spread her displeasure amongst the others as they came up to her.

'You needn't worry about *that* one,' Mam said, jerking her head towards Carmel. 'She'll be all right. She's a proper peasant. She has them as easy as shelling peas.' There was a trace of disgruntlement in her voice. (How much had her repeated bounties cost her over the years? And still without the desired results. It was a wonder she didn't give up—or allow Pat to.)

No one rose to the bait and Mam's gaze roved from face to face in growing dissatisfaction. None of them pleased her, although she didn't linger long on Bridie's. (Evidently, she still had not decided how to attack that situation.)

'I don't know,' she sighed. 'I just don't know what your father would have said if he were alive to see this day.'

'Well, you took care of that, didn't you?' Dee-Dee asked brutally.

'Oh, my heart!' (Briefly, Mam had wavered, the light of battle in her eyes again, before opting for her usual unanswerable routine.) 'My heart! You'll be the death of me yet!' She clutched a hand to her massive bosom and swayed.

Across the room, Carmel opened her eyes, new strength in her face. She assessed the situation and her eyes closed again, her lips moved soundlessly. '*No such luck,*' Eleanor read.

'Mam! Sit down quick!' Veronica was not able to treat the situation so lightly. (Of course, she had been conditioned from childhood.) 'Don't just stand there—' She glared at Dee-Dee and Bridie. '*Help* her!'

'There's nothing wrong with her,' Dee-Dee said. 'Except temper!'

'How *can* you?' Bridie was almost animated in her indignation. 'Here—' She moved forward to stand beside Veronica, who was nearly collapsing under the sag of Mam's full weight.

'Please, allow me—' James started to put an arm around Mam, lifting her weight off Veronica.

'You keep your dirty hands off me!' Mam sprang away from him.

'Oh, I say!' James was pained. 'I was only trying to help.'

'I don't need your help!' Mam snapped.

'And *that's* the truest word she's said in a long time,' Dee-Dee said. 'She's made a marvellous recovery, don't you think?'

'Ah, God!' Mam groaned, relapsing against Veronica. 'None of you care if I live or die.'

Veronica and Bridie protested immediately. Dee-Dee watched through narrowed eyes. James had backed away and was regarding the women nervously.

Eleanor knew better than to offer help. Mam would enjoy insulting her as she had insulted James—it would be foolish to give her the opportunity. Apart from which, it seemed to her that Carmel might be more immediately in need of aid. She crossed over to Carmel and spoke softly.

'How are you doing?'

'I'm coming round.' Carmel opened her eyes and grinned faintly. 'Though I'm not feeling as well as I was a minute ago when I thought the old besom might actually be having a seizure. It was silly of me to get so hopeful. Begod, the old bat will live for ever!'

'I'm afraid Veronica is more likely to come apart,' Eleanor agreed sombrely. 'The strain is beginning to tell on her.'

'She's put up with it for a long time,' Carmel said. 'She ought to get a medal.'

There were two thumps of great finality from overhead, and then utter silence. Until that moment, no one in the room had been wholly aware of the persistent struggle going on upstairs.

'Now what?' Carmel began to struggle to her feet. 'Begod, they're as bad as the kids. The minute they go quiet, you know nothing good can be happening.'

'I'll go,' Veronica said quickly. 'It can't be anything much.' The silence belied her words.

'Leave them alone!' Mam tottered as Veronica removed her support. '*They're* all right.' She sagged weakly to prove that *she* was not.

'Oh God!' Veronica wavered, head turning frantically from her mother to the doorway to the ceiling. Torn by the need to remain and the urge to discover what was happening upstairs, she seemed in danger of splitting in two. 'Oh my God!'

'Look—' Dee-Dee suggested compromise. 'Let's take Mam up to her room, and then we can see what those maniacs have done while we're up there.'

The atmosphere in the room lightened immediately, the prospect of getting rid of Mam cheering everyone. James moved forward again to help, but Mam shrank away.

'No!' she said. 'I'm not having *that* one in me bedroom.'

'It's all right,' Dee-Dee said to James. 'The three of us can manage.'

Dee-Dee on one side of Mam, Veronica on the other, with Bridie bringing up the rear, they left the room.

'Whew!' James looked across at Carmel and Eleanor, smiling his first genuine smile that evening. 'Dare one say that's a relief?'

'Dare away,' Carmel said. 'Begod, if I were in the condition for it, I'd go dancing around the room.'

'I'm afraid she's the mother-in-law to end all mothers-in-law,' Eleanor said. 'Especially to a Protestant in-law.'

'Yes.' James looked suddenly very thoughtful.

Eleanor wondered if this might be the right moment to suggest that it might be wiser not to move into the family orbit if it could possibly be avoided.

'In fact,' she began. 'I sometimes wish—'

A commotion broke out on the stairs outside. Amongst the hubbub, Eleanor recognized Kevin's voice and Mam's, but Terence's rose above all the others.

'Dee-Dee!' Terence cried. 'There you are! You've come to me, my darling. You've come!'

'Watch what you're doing!' Mam shrieked. 'Get away from me. Let me hold on to the stair rail. I'll fall, else!'

'No such luck,' Carmel muttered. But she was on her feet and racing towards the doorway with Eleanor and James.

'Get away!' Dee-Dee echoed. 'No! Let go! Stop it!'

'Terence!' Kevin thundered. 'Leave her alone!'

Dee-Dee screamed sharply. Mam screamed. There were shouts, thuds, more screams—and silence.

'What is it?' Carmel pushed Eleanor and James aside, getting through the doorway ahead of them, then stood frozen. Eleanor gently moved her to one side and stepped into the hallway, followed by James. Then she instantly wished that she had blocked James's view.

Dee-Dee lay crumpled at the foot of the stairs, her head and body twisted unnaturally.

'Dee-Dee!' Terence thrust his way past the knot of women huddled together in the middle of the staircase and leaped the remaining steps to Dee-Dee's side.

'Dee-Dee!' James charged forward to kneel beside Dee-Dee. He stretched out his hands, then pulled them back.

'Don't touch her,' Eleanor warned, as Terence stooped. 'You could do more harm than good. She—she may be badly hurt.' The twisted body made her words horribly apt—everyone recognized the truth of them.

'Dee-Dee—' James said again, softly. 'Darling—'

'Oh, James . . .' Dee-Dee's eyes fluttered open. It seemed to tap her last reserves of energy to speak. 'Oh, love, I wanted us to—'

'Don't talk,' James said. He took her hand gently. 'Just rest. You'll be all right—'

'Pushed me—' Dee-Dee's voice rose incredulously. '*Pushed* me downstairs . . . and I wanted us to have . . . such a happy life . . .' Her eyes closed.

'Get an ambulance!' James ordered 'Quickly!'

'Get a priest!' Mam countermanded. 'Hurry!'

But, before either could arrive, Dee-Dee died.

14.

'*Mickey* Concannon says it was a judgment on her.' Nicholas imparted the information between huge gulps of milk as lunch—or what passed for it next day—came to an end. 'Mickey Concannon says God struck Aunt Dee-Dee dead because she defied Him.'

'All right,' Kevin warned. 'That will be enough.'

'But Mickey Concannon says God was right,' Nicholas persisted. 'He says—'

'Please, Nicholas!' Eleanor put down her fork. She had only been using it to push the food around her plate anyway. Some day she and Kevin might get their appetites back—but not in the foreseeable future.

'Aunt Bridie says so, too.' Nicholas, revelling in a drama which had no reality for him, would not be halted. 'Aunt Bridie says—'

Kevin whirled on him and dealt him a back-handed blow.

Nicholas—so seldom even spanked—cried out in protest as much as pain, pushed back his chair and ran from the table in tears.

'I don't care what your Aunt Bridie says,' Kevin thundered after him. 'I don't care what your Mickey Concannon says! You'll mind your tongue about your Aunt Dee-Dee or I'll—I'll—' He broke off, sinking back into his chair, fighting to control tears of his own, so close to the surface.

'I'm sorry, Ellie.' After a moment, he glanced across the table at her, not quite meeting her eyes. 'Go after him, why don't you?'

'He'll be all right.' Torn between the desire to go after Nicholas and comfort him and the need to remain and solace Kevin—who, after all, was far more shocked and hurt than Nicholas—Eleanor sat tight and waited.

In her high chair, Margaret reacted belatedly to the atmosphere and began to cry in a soft, nerve-racking whine. Her world was awry, people weren't behaving properly. It frightened and upset her.

'Oh, for God's sake!' Kevin got up, flipped back the tray and released Margaret from the high chair. He picked her up and began to pace the room with her, burying his face in her neck. 'Don't *you* start. It's nothing to do with you, at all.' Their heads were so close together that Eleanor could not be sure that his tears were not mingling with Margaret's.

It was a time of tears, a house of tears. Inevitably there comes a death which transcends all others. A loss too poignant to be borne—except that there is nothing to be done except bear it. No escape, no evasion, no way out of the Stygian pit that has suddenly opened up and devoured the beloved, engulfed those remaining. One death which transcends all others. For Kevin, that death had come last night.

Last night. After the ambulance had gone, bearing away Dee-Dee's body; after the priest had dispensed what comfort he could and departed; after the doctor had seen to Mam, ministered to Terence, reassured Carmel that the shock—traumatic though it was—was not likely to hurt the child in her womb at this advanced stage; after the police had asked their questions and made their notes; after all that, she and

Kevin had returned home. Bridie, their pale and constant grey shadow, had returned with them.

Last night, when the lights were out, Kevin had lain in her arms and cried himself to sleep. Deep racking sobs that frightened her by their intensity, wrenched from a pit of anguish she was unable to share. She had genuinely liked Dee-Dee, but her own tears, she knew, were tears of sympathy rather than deep bereavement.

After Kevin had slept, worn out by the storm of his emotions, Eleanor had lain awake listening to the silence of the house, fear of some unidentified threat, some vague menace, shaking her until she had all she could do not to wake Kevin to reassure her. But sleep was the only reassurance, the only peace, Kevin himself could find right now. She could not rip it away from him.

Not moving, scarcely breathing, she had lain absolutely still, her mind busily trying to trace the course of her disquiet. Then, finally, she had it—and it frightened her more than the uncertainty.

It was the first night since her arrival that Bridie had *not* cried herself to sleep.

A subdued Carmel telephoned that afternoon. 'Can you come over?' she asked. 'No—no, I'm all right. I just don't feel like being alone just this minute, do you see? Don't laugh—' (although Eleanor had seen nothing amusing in the request.) 'I know I've got all the kids around me—but it's not the same.'

'I know,' Eleanor said. 'I'm feeling rather that way myself. I'll be over in a few minutes.'

Kevin and Pat had set off some time ago to 'make the arrangements'. Eleanor had not enquired into the specific nature of the 'arrangements' and Kevin had not volunteered the information. It was not through any intention of shielding her, she felt certain, it was rather that he did not understand that she might be in any doubt about what had to be done.

'There'll be the wake,' Carmel enlightened her, pouring tea. 'And the Requiem Mass. There's the cemetery plot to be seen to, and the—'

'But are they allowed to do any of that until after the Inquest?' ('It will be in two or three days,' the police had assured them smoothly, keeping official thoughts to themselves.)

'That's just a formality.' Carmel brushed it aside quickly. 'I rang Veronica this morning to see if there was anything I could do and—thank God—there wasn't.'

'Veronica—' Eleanor realized that she had had her own hands so full of problems that she had not given poor Veronica a thought. 'How is she?'

'Up the wall, of course. Mam's been creating. Terence woke up and started in drinking again right away. She hasn't seen James since he went off after the ambulance took Dee-Dee away last night. But all his things are in the house and he'll have to come back some time and she doesn't know what to say to him when he does. Mam's been insisting she pack his cases and leave them out on the steps for him to find when he gets back. Mam says she won't have him under her roof another five minutes.'

'It's Veronica's roof,' Eleanor pointed out. 'The house was left to her.'

'Try and convince Mam of that,' Carmel said. 'Veronica ought to have put her foot down and taken a tougher line about a lot of things a long time ago. I'm afraid it's too late now.'

'Mam's had her own way far too long,' Eleanor agreed. 'But I don't suppose this is the best time for Veronica to begin standing up to her.'

'No, this isn't the best time . . .' Carmel let the thought trail away. They sat in silence, trying to pretend that they weren't thinking of last night.

In the playpen, Margaret and Pegeen lay sleeping, curled together like a couple of kittens. Upstairs, Nicholas was playing with his cousins and collecting heaven knew how much more information and misinformation about the rites of Mother Church. (Well, sooner from them than from Mickey Concannon. A quiet word to Carmel later would go a long way towards sorting it all out.)

'I don't suppose—' Carmel began, and stopped.

Eleanor waited. Kevin had left the house without mentioning the subject. Over here, it seemed, the subject was being avoided, as well.

'Where's Bridie?' Carmel changed tack.

'I don't know,' Eleanor said shortly.

'And don't care,' Carmel finished for her. 'I don't blame you. All the same, I think we ought to keep an eye on her, so she doesn't go bothering Veronica. Poor Veronica has enough on her plate right now.'

'Is that the only reason we ought to keep an eye on Bridie?' Eleanor flung down the gauntlet and watched Carmel try to pretend it wasn't there.

'Oh, Ellie—' Carmel floundered. 'You don't—' The telephone bell saved her.

'I'll get it.' Eleanor rose, already feeling uneasy—if not guilty—about upsetting Carmel. The baby was dangerously close to due.

'Eleanor, is that you?' Veronica sounded frantic. 'Oh, thank heavens. I tried your number, but you weren't there, so I thought I'd have to make do with complaining to Carmel, and I didn't want to because she should be resting and taking it easy right now.'

Veronica sounded as though she could do with some rest herself. As for taking it easy, when had Veronica ever been able to do that? Working in an office all day and then coming home to pander to the whims of Mam evenings and weekends. Yes, and Terence, too. He took far more advantage of her good nature than a lodger ought, and probably seldom even thanked her for the spotless laundry, the freshly-ironed shirts, the favourite foods especially cooked, and all the extra comforts he took for granted.

'What's the matter, 'Ron?'

'Matter?' Veronica's laugh verged on the hysterical and was bitten off sharply. 'Oh, nothing. Nothing at all. Why should anything be the matter? Dee-Dee is dead. Terence is shut in his room drinking himself into a stupor and swearing that he's never going to set foot on those stairs again. Mam wants to throw James's things out of the house—and Bridie is offering to help her pack them—'

'So that's where Bridie is.' Eleanor kept her voice even, hoping it might have a calming effect on Veronica. 'Is she doing anything else? Anything helpful?'

'What do you expect?' Veronica's voice rose in a laugh that was half a sob. 'She's praying!'

'Veronica—' Eleanor tried not to sound as concerned as she felt. 'Why don't you slip over here for a few minutes. Come and have a cup of tea with us. Get out of that house for a little while.'

'I can't,' Veronica said despairingly.

'Of course you can,' Eleanor urged. 'Bridie's there. She can look after Mam—and Terence, too, if he should want anything.'

'I can't,' Veronica said again, and hung up abruptly.

Eleanor turned away from the phone slowly and met Carmel's eyes. They both shook their heads.

'I got the gist of that,' Carmel said. 'Though I couldn't hear Veronica's side—and I suspect that's just as well.'

'I suppose I ought to go over there,' Eleanor said reluctantly.

'Sooner you than me,' Carmel cheered her on. 'Finish your tea first.'

Eleanor resumed her seat and stared thoughtfully at her cup. Even Veronica, distraught as she was, obviously did not intend to raise the delicate subject. Was it to be totally ignored? Swept under the carpet and forgotten?

True, they had presented a united—and amnesiac—front to the police last night. But amongst themselves—Could anyone who had heard Dee-Dee's last words ever forget them?

'Veronica says that Terence is still shut in his room,' Eleanor approached the subject obliquely. 'Apparently, he's swearing that he'll never use those stairs again.'

'Veronica had better be careful.' Carmel shifted uncomfortably. 'If she starts pandering to that nonsense and doing anything silly, like taking dinner up to him, she could find herself carrying meals up those stairs for the rest of her life.'

'You don't really believe he's serious?' That sort of outcome had never occurred to Eleanor, but now that Carmel had mentioned it, she could see that it was well within the bounds of possibility.

'Who knows?' Carmel shrugged. 'At times, I think the Irish are *all* Nor'-Nor'-West. Just let the cold wind blow a bit too sharply from the wrong quarter and they're knocked off their perches—sometimes for good.'

'Then the sooner Veronica makes him face those stairs again, the better.' But would he? Was there a hidden reason for his intense over-reaction? (He had been struggling with Dee-Dee on the stairs. They had heard shouts and cries just before she fell. Fell—or was pushed? By Terence?)

'That's perfectly true.' Carmel refused to exchange glances. (Had the same thoughts been passing through *her* mind?) 'But Veronica's too soft with him. She lets him get away with—' Carmel stopped, aghast at what she had nearly said.

'Then you think so, too,' Eleanor said.

The doorbell saved Carmel from having to reply. She leaped up thankfully and dashed from the room, showing a turn of speed she usually only possessed between pregnancies.

Eleanor heard the front door open and then the sound of a male voice. She thought that Kevin and Pat must have returned, but there was something odd about the sound of the footsteps coming back down the hallway. Carmel's seemed to have lost their buoyancy.

When she appeared in the doorway, Eleanor saw, immediately behind her, the reason for those dragging footsteps. James stood there.

James. Gaunt, unshaven, haggard—a completely different man to the one Dee-Dee had introduced so proudly as her fiancé. Just barely recognizable as James.

'Look who's here,' Carmel said bleakly.

'James.' Eleanor greeted him uneasily. 'How *are* you?'

'I've just left Dee-Dee,' he said. 'That is—' he looked around, blinking—'I don't know when I left her. I've been walking around for hours, trying to think—'

'Sit down.' Carmel pulled out a chair. 'Have a cup of tea.'

'Thank you.' James dropped into the chair, but did not seem to notice the cup of tea Carmel poured.

'Have you been back to the house yet?' Eleanor asked cautiously.

'No. I couldn't.' He raised his head, his haunted eyes stared across the table at her. 'I couldn't go into that hallway . . . look at those stairs . . . *use* them— No!'

'No,' Eleanor agreed.

'Besides,' James added. 'I couldn't stay in that house now.'

'I quite see that.' (But surely James wouldn't leave before the funeral? In that case, where was he to stay? Now that Mam knew the worst, would Bridie agree to moving over there and letting James have her room? Even if it were only temporary, the respite from having her around would—)

'I'll go to a hotel,' James said.

'That might be best,' Carmel encouraged. 'That way, you could come and go as you liked until the funeral, and afterwards you'll be able to leave without any awkwardness.' Something in James's expression caused her to break off abruptly.

'Leave?' James looked at her strangely. 'Oh no, I'm not leaving.'

'But you'll have to get back to your job. And you won't want that transfer up here, after all that's happened. There's no reason for you to stay around—'

'There *is* a reason,' James said softly. 'Dee-Dee is dead—and it's someone's fault. I want to avenge her.'

15.

' "*Vengeance* is mine, saith the Lord," ' Carmel protested feebly.

'Justice, then.' James turned his burning eyes on her and she looked away.

'Oh, but—' Eleanor began. The incandescent eyes slashed across her, cutting her off.

'*You* were there,' James said. '*You* heard her.'

Eleanor looked away. Those eyes were more than she could meet. He had not wept, like Kevin, last night. It would have been healthier for him if he had.

'Dee-Dee is dead,' James said. His voice was wild, bereft. 'Gone.' He took a deep breath. 'She *can't* go—not just like that. Dee-Dee. So happy, so alive. She—she can't just be *over*. *Ended*—and no one will *do* anything. No one will—' His voice broke.

Eleanor and Carmel exchanged a despairing look. James was oblivious of them both now, obviously fighting for control. (Where was Kevin? Where was Pat? Why didn't they return?)

'I'm going to tell the truth at the Inquest,' James said abruptly. 'And I want both of you to do the same.'

'What?' The protest was simultaneous. Eleanor and Carmel met each other's eyes with even greater consternation. This was worse than they had feared.

'You were both there,' James persisted. 'You heard what Dee-Dee said. Someone pushed her. Killed her.'

'Oh, but she couldn't have known what she was saying,' Carmel protested. 'She was stunned, dazed—'

'She was dying!' James said harshly.

'Oh, dear God!' Carmel moaned.

'It was an accident,' Eleanor said. 'It *must* have been.'

'Do you honestly believe that?'

'Yes.' Eleanor looked away. (Surely those eyes would haunt her dreams for years to come. They would float disturbingly at the edge of pleasant dreams, pursue her relentlessly through nightmares.)

'I see.' His voice was bitter. 'So that's the way it's going to be. I thought you people would help me.'

'Well, of course, we would,' Carmel said. 'If we thought it would do any good.'

'It won't bring Dee-Dee back, I know.' James brooded into his untasted cup of tea.

'And—there's the scandal—' Carmel grasped at the straw she imagined she glimpsed. 'We have the children to think of—'

'You'd rather have them living in the same street with a murderer.' James raised his frightening eyes again. 'You'd rather have them visit their grandmother, knowing there's a killer under her roof, than risk facing scandal. And you—' He turned his gaze on Eleanor. 'Are you quaking with terror about what the neighbours might say?'

'Certainly not.' (The spectre of Mrs Concannon twitching aside her lace curtain to stare with unconcealed glee at the fall of the mighty rose at the back of Eleanor's mind. She tried to ignore it.)

'But, if we say one thing . . .' she faltered on . . . 'and the others deny it . . .' (Visions of a family divided by a lifelong feud flooded her mind now.) 'And Dee-Dee *couldn't* have meant it. She was mistaken. It *must* have been an accident.' She was talking too fast, trying to justify herself now. 'Even if it wasn't, it's the sort of thing that would be hard to prove. Almost impossible, I'd think.'

'So you'd let him get away with murder, too.' James turned away from them both. He looked terrifyingly lost and alone—but even more terrifyingly determined.

'What are you going to do?' Carmel asked uneasily.

'If necessary, I shall tell the truth by myself at the Inquest.' James squared his shoulders. 'Perhaps you're right and no one will believe me—with all of you aligned against me. If not, then I shall be forced to consider other alternatives.'

'I think the police have to have some sort of proof,' Eleanor said. (Surely James wasn't going to start a vendetta all by himself?) 'I'm sure they can't act without it.'

'Than you won't back me up?'

'We didn't even see anything,' Carmel said desperately. 'Always providing there was anything to see.'

'Perhaps it *was* too much to expect you to give evidence,' James said. 'I thought perhaps, since you weren't really members of the family, except by marriage . . . I can see that I was wrong. I shouldn't have asked it of you. But I couldn't go to any of the others . . .'

'No, you couldn't,' Carmel agreed. She stared into space with morbid fascination, as though seeing Mam's reactions to an accusation of murder under her roof. 'But wasn't last night the time to have said something? When the police were there anyway and asking questions?'

'We should have—' James glanced at them and corrected himself. '*I* should have. But I wasn't thinking coherently. I couldn't believe she was really dead. It didn't seem possible. I kept thinking that the ambulance men would bring her round any moment and all my thoughts, my attention—I was concentrating on them. Nothing else.'

'Naturally,' Carmel nodded. 'But, you see, if we were all to change our stories now, it would look—'

'You've made your point.' James pushed back his chair and rose. 'I'm sorry to have bothered you. Please forget that I asked.'

'Wait a minute.' Eleanor was loath to see him go off in such a mood. (Where might he go? What might he do?)

'Yes?' James paused politely, disinterestedly, waiting for her to continue.

'You don't really believe Terence would do a thing like that?' she pleaded. (But she already half-believed it herself. Terence, as they had all seen, was not quite sane about Dee-Dee—and Dee-Dee had made it very plain that he could abandon all hope.)

'Don't you?' He threw it back to her.

'But he wouldn't. He loved her. And Terence is really so kind and gentle—' She broke off at the look on his face.

'You really don't know anything about it, do you?' he asked wonderingly. He looked at Carmel, who was staring at him blankly. 'Nor do you.'

'Know about what?' Carmel seemed to force the words out.

'The past.' He said the words calmly, emotionlessly. There was no reason why they should cause both women to shiver. Yet they did. It was as thought the past were a grim, chill spectre which had been stalking them silently since—since Bridie had come home, bringing all the echoes and memories of the past with her.

'You heard some of the other things Dee-Dee said earlier in the evening,' James pressed on relentlessly. 'Don't you remember that she said she wouldn't testify against Terence? What did you *think* she meant by that?'

'We didn't think anything at all,' Carmel admitted. 'She'd been saying a lot of things that obviously only made sense to her and Terence—'

'She meant just what she said,' James told them. 'That even though she was no longer married to him, she couldn't be forced to give evidence against him—and she wouldn't.'

'Evidence about what?' Eleanor asked.

'Ten years ago.' James still seemed faintly incredulous. 'Dee-Dee told me all about it.'

'Well, nobody told *us*,' Carmel assured him.

'Perhaps they wouldn't,' James admitted. 'If you didn't know anything about it to begin with, I can see that it would have been better to have kept you out of it.' He sat down again and looked at them thoughtfully.

'Ten years ago,' Carmel prompted. 'That would have been when Dee-Dee eloped with Terence.'

'And Bridie went into the convent.' Eleanor followed the sequence of events most pertinent to her own problems.

'All of that,' James agreed. 'And that was when the old man—Dee-Dee's father—died, too, if you remember.'

'No—' Carmel had gone pale—'I'd forgotten that.' But a desolate light in her eyes betrayed that she had not forgotten—she had simply avoided connecting it with the other events.

'Had you?' James was not going to let her off easily. 'And you—' he turned to Eleanor—'had you forgotten, too?'

'It was before we were married,' Eleanor said. 'I knew *what* had happened, but I never knew—'

'Why—or how,' James finished for her. He turned back to Carmel. 'And is that *your* story, as well?'

'It's the truth,' Carmel said. 'Pat was upset enough to make the angels weep, but he wouldn't talk about it. From that day to this, he's never uttered a word.'

'And you've never asked?' James pressed home the indictment.

'No.' Carmel raised her head and looked at him proudly. 'A man has the right to keep certain things to himself. There are some questions I've never asked.'

'Kevin seldom spoke of his family during that time,' Eleanor said. 'I knew there was trouble— sadness—in the family, but by the time he introduced me to everyone, it was all over. Bridie had already gone into the convent. And Dee-Dee and Terence had married and split up soon after—it didn't last long.'

'How could it, considering the circumstances? Oh, Dee-Dee was a bit wild, as a girl,' James said defensively. 'She never attempted to deny that. Given her upbringing any girl would have been. It was nothing to hold against her.'

'Sure not,' Carmel agreed, watching him expectantly.

'She was a student,' James said. 'Naturally, she got involved with politics. They were all in it—all the girls—Dee-Dee, Veronica and Bridie. You can see, the way they were brought up, that it would seem glamorous to them. Something worth doing—for a Cause.'

'Oh no,' Carmel moaned. 'Not the Cause again! I've heard about it all my life and I'm sick of it—and of all the idiots who gibber about it. Do you mean to tell me that the girls were mixed up in it?'

'Up to their necks,' James said. 'Their mother encouraged them. Actively supported them.'

'The old besom!'

'They were young,' James defended his beloved. 'It wasn't real to them. It was excitement, intrigue. Death didn't come into it—not at first. They didn't begin to realize what they were doing until it was almost too late.'

'But Kevin—' Eleanor said incredulously. 'Kevin and Pat. What about them? Didn't *they* know what was going one?'

'Dee-Dee thinks they didn't want to know. They were older and had their own lives opening out before them. She even thought at the time that it was rather selfish of them to be more interested in going out and having a good time. Later, she wished that she'd done the same.'

'Pat was courting me in those days,' Carmel said thoughtfully. 'I used to wonder why I didn't see more of his family—if he was really serious about me. Sometimes, it seemed he was deliberately keeping me away from them. When I first met his mother, I thought I understood the reason.'

'The boys worried but, with their mother encouraging the whole thing and treating the girls like heroines, there wasn't much they could do. They protested on occasion, but the girls wouldn't listen to them.'

'I knew Pat was a worried man a lot of the time,' Carmel said. 'But I thought it was because he was making up his mind to take on the responsibilities of marriage.'

'At first it was just courier work—the usual thing.' James's eyes were inward-looking, perhaps remembering the story as Dee-Dee had first told it to him. 'They carried messages and small parcels when they went to Ireland on holidays. They were tourists, innocent-looking, pretty. Customs had no reason to suspect them. They got away with it. Then, gradually, they got in deeper.'

'Didn't I once hear—' a faint recollection stirred in Eleanor's mind—'that they met Terence on holiday in Ireland?'

'He came back to England with them and organized them into a cell.' James was grim, but trying to be fair. 'It was still fun for them—a big adventure.

Terence wasn't that much older or more sophisticated, either. They weren't much more than
children—playing games. It hadn't really got through
to them that they could hurt, maim, even kill people
with their games.'

'*Some* of them didn't realize it,' Carmel said darkly.

'Yes,' James nodded. 'Bridie was the ringleader.'

'She would be.' Eleanor found that she was not
surprised. Even today there was something about
Bridie which hinted at a seething turmoil beneath the
surface irreconcilable with any genuine love of
God—or of her fellow-man.

'She deferred to Terence, of course. They all did.
Dee-Dee used to say—' James clenched his jaw—'that
was when she first began paying attention to Terence.
Because she was so sorry for him. She knew Bridie
didn't give a tinker's curse for him—except as the
contact who could get arms and ammunition for
them. And Terence—at first—had eyes for no one
but Bridie. Because she was so dedicated. He thought
he'd found a lifelong partner and they'd go down the
years together—serving the Cause. Perhaps Bridie
thought the same. When he proposed, she accepted
and everything seemed set fair for the future. But the
real driving spirit was Mam.'

'Mam,' Carmel echoed. 'Begod, it was the wrong
parent who died in that accident, I'm thinking. I've
always thought so.'

'That accident—' Eleanor looked at James enquir-
ingly.

'Their father seems to have been a decent sort,'
James said. 'They were all fond of him—Dee-Dee
especially. But he was overwhelmed and overshad-
owed by his wife. It's pretty obvious he had no idea of
what she was up to, nor that she'd pulled the girls into
the mess along with her. When he found out—'

'Do you mean it wasn't an accident?' Carmel was

prepared to believe anything of Mam. 'Do you mean that Mam—?'

'Up to that point, they'd done nothing too serious,' James said. 'Remembering that the IRA wasn't an outlawed group in those days. Membership may have been officially frowned upon, but it wasn't forbidden. And they were very much on the fringes.

'But Bridie had been pushing Terence to make the powers-that-be give them a real assignment. No matter whether the others thought they were ready for it or not—or even whether they really felt that committed to the Cause. Bridie was—and that was all that counted. Dee-Dee always said that Bridie secretly longed for martyrdom.'

'She's likely to get it,' Carmel muttered. 'She's driving Veronica as frantic now as she's been driving Eleanor.'

'Poor Veronica.' James seemed totally in accord with the rest of them on that subject. 'She was always the best of the lot, I gather—apart from Dee-Dee.'

'But what happened?' Eleanor scorned the digression.

'Bridie came down the 'flu,' James said. 'Just as the higher-ups agreed that their cell had earned its right to take a more active part in what was being planned. Terence and Bridie had been scheduled to meet someone and drive back to England with him, pretending to be one family. It was called "Escort Duty". But Bridie came down with the 'flu. Instead, Terence and Dee-Dee went over.'

It was as real and vivid to James, Eleanor saw, as though it had happened yesterday. Perhaps because, while he was telling it, Dee-Dee was alive again. Going back into her past enabled him to keep at bay the knowledge of what her future had come to.

'They got to know each other on that journey.' James was still safely locked in the past, even the jealousy radiating from him providing an insulation.

'At lease, they imagined they did—two heroes of the Cause! It was the original mutual admiration society.

'And their contact was three days late at the rendezvous. They had that much longer together, wondering what they should do if he didn't turn up, worrying about what might be happening. In each other's company constantly, with no one else to turn to—'

James broke off. The past had abruptly become more than he wanted to face, either. Eleanor and Carmel exchanged dismayed glances. (What would they do if he broke down completely?)

'Back at the house,' James took a deep breath and continued, 'Dee-Dee's absence hadn't been very well explained. Their father began to ask some very pointed questions. He wasn't satisfied with the answers he got. He kept on at them. Mam stopped speaking to him, Bridie took refuge in her illness but, eventually, Veronica cracked and told him what had been going on.

'He set off immediately to find Dee-Dee and bring her home. He was in such a fury that not even Mam dared try to stop him.'

Carmel nodded appreciatively. Unlike Eleanor, she had met Pat's father and this evidently accorded with her assessment of him. Like many mild men, he could rise to heights of righteous fury daunting to those who had previously underestimated him.

'Their father realized more of the situation than the girls did,' James went on. 'Perhaps because he'd been living around it for so much of his life. He'd been in places they couldn't go and, amongst his workmates, in Irish pubs, he'd heard whispers, rumours, threats. He knew how to interpret the whispering—and the sudden silences. He knew what "Escort Duty" meant.

'He knew that militant action was being planned for the future, and that foreign agitators and even professional criminals had been recruited and were being brought into England to teach their methods of death and destruction to the sleeper cells. He knew they were also shipping in and stock-piling arms, ammunition—and gelignite—against the day they'd suddenly attack an unprepared community.

'He knew—and he didn't approve. But he didn't do anything until he discovered how far his own daughters had been dragged into it.'

'Glory be to God!' Carmel said. 'No wonder he exploded!'

'Yes—' James looked at her thoughtfully, almost suspiciously. 'In the end, that was literally what he did.'

'Literally—?' Eleanor found that she wished she could stop listening. She did not want to hear what James was about to divulge next.

'He caught up with Dee-Dee and Terence at that little hotel just as their contact arrived with the car and passenger they were to drive back to England— via Northern Ireland.

'Dee-Dee couldn't believe it when her father told her what they were really being tricked into doing— neither could Terence. As I said, they were very young—and the world has learned a lot more about political realities since those days.

'To prove it, Dee-Dee's father rushed out to the car that had been provided and began to search it while the contact and the agitator tried to stop him, all the while denying everything to Dee-Dee and Terence.

'Then her father lifted out the back seat and pulled out a rifle—

'That was enough for Dee-Dee. Probably for Terence, too,' James admitted grudgingly. 'Although Terence didn't say anything, and he didn't even go to help the old boy. I think that was really the beginning of the end—that Terence wouldn't move to help her father—and that he kept Dee-Dee from going to help.

'They were both stunned. It was all more than they had bargained for. Suddenly, it had stopped being good clean fun and excitement.

'Dee-Dee heard her father shout, "There's gelignite here, too!" But then the other two jumped into the car and drove off—with him still in the back. Dee-Dee saw her father straighten up and then hurl himself over the front seat, struggling to get at the steering-wheel.

'The car swerved, ran off the road—sideswiped a tree—and then exploded—'

James fell silent again, staring into the distance, seeing the scene through Dee-Dee's eyes, echoing Dee-Dee's emotions.

'It was all hushed up, of course. It happened in an area where there were plenty of sympathizers. Someone telephone England and Mam rushed over, leaving Veronica to nurse Bridie. Dee-Dee was in a state of shock, and Terence was frightened out of what wits he had—they were puppets in the hands of those others. And, of course, there was a great deal of moral blackmail involved, as well.

'All Mam was worried about was the neighbours. Dee-Dee and Terence had been missing for nearly a week and people were beginning to talk. Now, with a dead husband on her hands, it would be even worse. She went along with the suggestions that came down from the High Command.

'They buried him in an old churchyard in Eire, where some of his ancestors lay. Dee-Dee and Terence were hustled into a church and married quickly and quietly.' James's fists clenched. 'It couldn't be a Registry Office—oh no, Mam was afraid of "giving scandal" to the neighbours. She had to tie them together "in the eyes of the Church". So that now, Dee-Dee and I——' He broke off abruptly, looking stricken, as though realizing that he had slipped into the present tense, when it was all past tense now. Dee-Dee and all their plans were past tense, too.

'Thanks be to God,' Carmel muttered in a grateful undertone. She was facing the window. 'Here come Pat and Kevin.'

'When they got back to England—' fighting for control, James went on—'the story was given out that there'd been an elopement, and that Dee-Dee's father had died in a car crash—the inference being that he had been chasing the elopers at the time. It was close enough to the truth to be believable, once they were married, and contained just enough hint of scandal to satisfy the more suspicious neighbours. No one cared what it did to Dee-Dee.'

With a gratitude to equal Carmel's, Eleanor heard the front door open and slow footsteps sombrely marching down the hall in measured tread, as though Pat and Kevin were unconsciously rehearsing their coming role as pall-bearers.

'Terence was madly in love with Dee-Dee by this time. Naturally.' It was the one thing about Terence that James could understand. 'But it didn't take Dee-Dee long to come to her senses and leave him. Even then, he wouldn't accept it. He followed her, pestered her, until she had to move to another city. Even after the divorce, he still wouldn't let her go. He drove her nearly insane. Finally, she moved to London and cut all ties with her family.

'She should have kept away—' James's voice was agonized. 'She should never have come back. I should have known better than to let her. I should have realized the extent of his madness. I should have—'

'There was nothing you could have done,' Carmel broke in comfortingly. 'You weren't to know. Not even Dee-Dee guessed and, God knows, she had more reason to than you.'

Pat and Kevin were framed in the doorway, hesitating, groggy as punch-drunk prizefighters, listening, trying to take in the meaning of the scene before them. One more scene in a life which had abruptly and cruelly become a procession of incredible scenes.

'He's going to pay,' James said. 'It isn't going to be hushed up this time. Not Dee-Dee. I know the way he thought: *"If I can't have her, no one will"*. It's classic with men of his type. The crime passionel. But it's Dee-Dee he killed. *Dee-Dee!*' The voice wavered out of control again.

'And I won't let him get away with it. I'm going to see that Terence pays. And you'll help me, won't you?' he appealed to Eleanor and Carmel. 'You'll stand up at the Inquest with me and testify—'

'No, they won't!' Pat said from the doorway. James turned in surprise.

'But, Pat—' Carmel was wavering, half-convinced of her duty.

'They won't,' Pat said again. 'Terence didn't do it.'

'He didn't?' Eleanor lifted an eyebrow at Kevin.

'He didn't.' Kevin came into the room and slumped into a chair heavily. 'We'd pulled him away from Dee-Dee, you remember. He was struggling with us to get back to her, and we were both holding him as tight as we could when she fell.

'Do you think—' his voice rose—'do you think we'd have seen him harm one hair of Dee-Dee's head and not have torn him limb from living limb?'

16.

In the silence that followed, they all avoided looking at one another. Carmel rose clumsily, giving Pat her chair, and hurried to pour tea for the newcomers, although their breath betrayed that they had stopped for stronger sustenance elsewhere along the way. James seemed lost in thought, perhaps grappling with the implications of the information just received—or perhaps simply denying it altogether.

Eleanor looked at Kevin, but he was leaning back in his chair, eyes closed. (Because he was overcome with emotion? Because he was exhausted by the necessary tasks he and Pat had been performing? Or simply because he had been lying about Terence?)

Carmel put down the teapot, looking so ill that Eleanor hastily got to her feet and pushed her into the vacated chair. 'No—' she silenced Carmel's protest. 'You sit there—I'll get another chair.' It was with relief that she escaped into the living-room to find a chair for herself. The atmosphere in the kitchen had suddenly become more than she could endure.

Upstairs, there was the sound of children at subdued play, consciously stifling their natural spirits in deference to the strange recent events, and the even stranger way they affected the grown-ups.

She sank into the chair thoughtfully for a moment

(just for a moment, she promised herself), reluctant to return to the kitchen. There was a silence out there which conveyed a sense of brooding rather than peace. (How could there be peace again for any of them? They knew too much, and yet not enough.)

It was an impossible situation. Impossible for James—who desperately needed someone to blame, to be revenged upon—to admit that Dee-Dee's last words might have been wrong, that she might have been mistaken, or perhaps even unaware that she had spoken.

And yet, Terence had been ruled out. He would have fitted so beautifully and, basically, James was correct. Terence *did* have the mentality to have acted on an '*If I can't have her, no one will*' basis. But Pat and Kevin had been holding him tightly when Dee-Dee plunged down the stairs, indisputable witnesses to his innocence.

What would James do now? Would he accept that, since Terence had nothing to do with Dee-Dee's death, it must have been an accident? He had to accept it. The alternative was unthinkable.

Unthinkable to them, but not perhaps to James. The silence in the kitchen was a strong indication that every one of them was now brooding upon the alternative.

If Terence hadn't pushed Dee-Dee, that left Mam, Bridie and Veronica. Would James next accuse one of them?

If he did, she ought to be out there to weigh in on the family side with protests. Sighing faintly (she seemed to have done quite a lot of sighing since Bridie first descended upon them), Eleanor stood, picked up her chair and returned to the kitchen with it.

The noise as she put down the chair seemed to startle James out of what might have been a trance.

'It wasn't an accident.' James looked from one to

another, having caught the thought in the air and intent on denying it.

'It must have been,' Pat insisted stubbornly.

'It wasn't.' James stared him down. 'Dee-Dee said so. Dee-Dee said she was pushed.'

'Where does that leave us then?' Carmel looked older than her years, exhausted—guilty, even. If Eleanor had not been with her every moment, had not rushed into the hallway with her, been at her side when they found Dee-Dee lying at the foot of the stairs—

Eleanor wrenched her mind away from the thought. (She must look guilty herself now.) 'Dee-Dee *must* have been mistaken,' she said faintly. (She had said it before—or Carmel had. They had all said it before. They were trapped in some nightmare where they would go on saying the same things over and over again, convincing no one. Perhaps not even themselves.)

'Do you really believe that?' It might have been a challenge had he used a different tone, but he asked it indifferently, as though realizing that he would never get a truthful answer from any of them. His eyes were abstracted—perhaps he was beginning to realize the full implications of continuing with his accusation.

Mam . . . Bridie . . . Veronica. Could *he* believe that one of them had done such a thing?

In the playpen, Margaret whimpered, waking up. Eleanor went over and picked her up, burying her face in the baby's hair, hiding her expression lest Kevin be able to read it.

She could believe that Mam would do such a thing. She could even guess at the justification Mam would use to herself: '*I brought her into the world, I have the right to send her out of it.*' She had always been aware that there was something of the monster about Mam. Mam had tried to deny too many human rights to her

children. To Mam, the children she had borne were
not entitled to any life of their own—away from her.
Mam had never looked on them as human beings,
simply as pawns—to be discarded if and when their
usefulness to her had ended.

'Let the woman die . . .' Dee-Dee had escaped
Mam's domination and built a life of her own. But
Dee-Dee had returned, bringing what Mam thought
of as scandal with her. Worse—Eleanor remembered
the veiled remarks which now took on new
meanings—Dee-Dee had threatened to re-open an
old scandal, to move back into the neighbourhood to
be a constant reminder of an episode everyone would
prefer closed. And so, Dee-Dee had died.

Veronica— But Veronica had been on the far side
of Mam and Bridie. On the outside, as she had been
on the outside fringes of earlier events. Apart from
which, Veronica had been genuinely fond of Dee-
Dee.

Which was more than one could say of Bridie.
Eleanor had been trying to avoid the thought of
Bridie altogether. (Because Bridie was still a guest in
her home? Because it was terrifying to imagine a
murderess under the same roof as Nicholas and
Margaret?)

Bridie— Eleanor glanced at Carmel, but Carmel
was looking blankly at her empty teacup, absorbed in
thought. Thoughts which could not be very different
from Eleanor's own.

Bridie. It was only too possible. Bridie was plainly,
if not an outright religious maniac, then certainly a
neurotic of no mean proportions. She had—despite
her parade of meekness—shown deep resentment
more than once at certain irreverent remarks of
Dee-Dee's. There was a dangerous instability about
Bridie which made any suspicion not so ill-founded as
it might have been.

(Had Bridie entered the convent in expiation for

the death of her father—or because she considered that she had failed the Cause? Had Bridie really left the convent for the reason given—or had there been a deeper, darker reason, as Carmel had suggested?)

'What are you going to do?' Carmel asked again.

'I don't know,' James said slowly. 'It doesn't really change anything.' His face hardened. '*Someone* pushed Dee-Dee.'

'You realize you're talking now about her own mother.' Pat's face was hard, too. 'Or her sister.'

'Yes,' James said. 'I realize that.'

'Why are we talking like this?' Kevin tried a smile that bore no relation to the expression in his eyes. 'It was an accident. We all know that. It has to be.' The smile faded as he looked around at their shuttered faces.

'*Has* to be?' James echoed. 'Why don't we all tell the truth at the Inquest and let the authorities decide?'

What would they decide? Eleanor wondered fleetingly whether it would go down into the statistics as another domestic murder or a sectarian killing.

'We can't,' Carmel pleaded desperately. 'We can't wash our dirty linen in public. Think what it would do to the children.'

'Think what it did to Dee-Dee,' James said.

'Let's not rush into anything,' Pat temporized. 'Let's just take it easy for a bit, think things over, remember everything that was said and done. Kevin and I were right there, you know, and *we* couldn't swear she'd been pushed, so how could you say it when you came out after it had happened?'

'*You* wouldn't say it, even if you'd seen it. Oh—' James cut off Pat's protest. 'You can talk about tearing Terence apart, but you wouldn't touch your mother.'

'More's the pity,' Carmel muttered under her breath, fortunately unheard by the men. Of course, Carmel had good reason to expect the worst of Mam. Eleanor let her gaze trail thoughtfully around the kitchen—Carmel had a new fridge, too—and there had been a discussion about adding a new room to the house. (Because it was really needed, or because it would be conspicuously cocking a snook at this year's unsuccessful attempt to rid herself of a daughter-in-law?)

Or would it be so unsuccessful? Looking at Carmel's wan face, Eleanor felt an uneasy pang. Perhaps these continual pregnancies were taking more toll than Carmel imagined. (But Mam, after five of her own, would know.)

Another thought—so disquieting that Eleanor immediately tried to thrust it from her—slid into her mind and refused to be dislodged.

Having once killed, would Mam—or Bridie—kill again? Was Carmel destined to be the next victim?

Mam, because she had always resented Carmel for marrying and holding on to her eldest son. Because she had, in a devious way, already been trying to get rid of Carmel.

Bridie because, having tilted over into the excesses of religious mania enough to murder a sister who had, as she saw it, profaned the Faith, she would consider it a logical extension of piety to rid the world of yet another who did not take the Faith seriously enough. And, God knows, Carmel, with her cheerful blasphemies, had occasioned more than one gasp of shocked horror from Bridie.

Margaret whimpered and stirred restlessly in Eleanor's arms. Not for the first time, she was aware that a child could provide the most civilized excuse for escaping an awkward situation.

'Really, dear—' she spoke across the others to Kevin, including him in her escape—'I think we ought to get the children home. They've had an exhausting day.'

And so have we, Kevin's answering nod agreed. 'I'll call Nicholas.' He moved towards the front hall.

'Where are you going?' Pat snapped. But it was not to Kevin he spoke.

James had taken advantage of the diversion to rise from his chair and start for the door. Kevin halted and turned towards James. For a moment, both he and Pat looked dangerous.

'Back to the hospital,' James said. 'Even if they won't let me in, I . . . I want to be near Dee-Dee.'

Kevin bowed his head and turned away.

17.

Kevin carrying Margaret, they returned to their own house in a silent procession. Eleanor opened the door (she hadn't locked it) and led the way into the living-room. In the doorway, she halted abruptly.

There was a recumbent form on the sofa. For a heart-fluttering moment, she knew fresh fear, then saw the slow rise and fall of Veronica's bosom.

Veronica had simply fallen asleep. In the crook of her arm, Furface curled purring, delighted that someone had the time again to provide a comfortable napping spot.

'Shhh . . .' Eleanor started to back away before they awakened Veronica, but it was too late. Furface opened her eyes and chirruped a pleased welcome. Nicholas started forward. Furface stretched luxuriously and marched across Veronica's stomach to meet him.

'Wha-at—?' Veronica started and sat up blinking. Her glasses slid from her hand to the floor. Still not quite awake, Veronica groped for them, her eyes seeming paler and smaller, framed by dark circles.

Vulnerable. Veronica had always seemed vulnerable and now, without her glasses, she seemed more so than ever.

'Go back to sleep, 'Ron,' Kevin said gently. 'It's all

right. We didn't mean to wake you. We just didn't know you were here.'

'I'm sorry.' Veronica found her glasses and slipped them on, still blinking. 'I didn't mean to fall asleep. You weren't here and I thought I'd just stretch out for a minute.'

'It's all right,' Kevin assured her.

'Suddenly, I *had* to get out of that house for a little while.' Veronica continued her apology, directing it to Eleanor now. 'And it's always so peaceful here—'

It *had* been. Until the advent of Bridie. Once Bridie had left, it might be again.

'I'll make tea.' Eleanor began a retreat.

'Forget that.' Kevin stopped her. 'She needs a *real* drink.' He transferred Margaret into her arms and went into the kitchen.

'I don't want to be any bother,' Veronica protested feebly. 'I ought to be getting back.' She looked at her watch. 'I've been gone longer than I intended. I must have been asleep for half an hour. They'll be wondering where I am.'

'Let them wonder.' Kevin had returned, carrying a tray. 'You needed the rest. It will do you good.' He thrust a drink into her hand. 'So will this.'

'Yes.' Veronica sipped at it doubtfully.

'You worry too much about other people. You should think of yourself more.' It was scarcely the time for fraternal homilies, but Kevin was undoubtedly feeling guilty for allowing Veronica to shoulder too much of the burden of Mam.

'It's a nightmare!' Veronica's hand began trembling abruptly, threatening to spill her drink. 'I keep thinking I'll wake up and find it was all a bad dream, but—' She set the drink down carefully on the table beside the sofa and blinked once more—this time because her eyes were brimming with sudden tears.

'Here you are.' Kevin had brought a Coke for Nicholas. 'And you.' Eleanor's drink was such a dark amber that she was certain there would be no water in it until the ice cubes began to melt.

'What I really came over for—' Veronica fought for control. 'I—We . . . wanted to know what . . . what arrangements . . . have been made.' The tears were perilously close once more.

'Nicholas,' Eleanor said. 'Take Furface out—'

'No,' Kevin said, 'let him stay.' *He'll have to learn*, the look he gave her said.

Why? Why should a child like Nicholas have to learn about such things? But the answer came immediately: because some day it would be *his* turn to make the arrangements. For herself, or for Kevin, or both. Life flowed swiftly, and Nicholas would not remain a child for ever, nor would she and Kevin remain young and strong and alive. *'In the midst of life . . .'*

Eleanor took a long swallow of her own drink and found that it was not overstrong after all.

'They'll release the body after the Inquest—' Kevin skated over the thin ice quickly, not meeting any eyes. 'Then we'll wake her at O'Meara's Funeral Parlour, and we'll have the Solemn Requiem Mass on—'

Margaret began to wail, squirming to be put down.

'She needs to be changed,' Eleanor said thankfully and withdrew. At least Margaret was too young to know what was going on and could be protected for a few more years. (But how much protection would there be for her if James had his way? Even though the accusation might be disproved, rumours would circulate around the family for long years ahead. Margaret would meet those rumours in school. There would be veiled hints, if not outright taunts. What protection would there be against that?)

When she came back downstairs, carrying a clean and cooing Margaret, Veronica had left. Kevin sat in the living-room, brooding into his drink, and a subdued

Nicholas was pouring out milk for Furface in the kitchen. No one seemed in the mood for further conversation, so Eleanor busied herself with preparations for the next meal, although it was unlikely that anyone would notice, or particularly care, if she skipped it altogether.

When she heard the front door close, Eleanor thought at first that Kevin had gone out. But Furface lifted her head, looked in the direction of the sound, then folded back her ears and disappeared under the stove. Eleanor was not surprised when Bridie came into the kitchen.

'There you are,' Bridie greeted, eyes darting around the room swiftly before she hooded them and dropped her gaze to her clasped hands.

'Here I am,' Eleanor agreed. Nicholas had backed warily into a corner, looking as though he wished he could join Furface under the stove.

'I shan't want anything to eat,' Bridie said. 'I've just come back to get my missal and rosary. I'm taking Mam to church.'

'Fine.' Eleanor tried to inject some proper enthusiasm into the comment, but suspected that her relief showed. Every moment that Bridie was out of the house was a reprieve.

'How is Mam taking it?' The question was prompted by guilt. (Should she have ignored the dictum that Mam was prostrated and gone over to visit?)

'Oh, quite well.' Bridie nodded complacently. 'Quite well. She understands that it was really for the best.'

Best for whom? Eleanor turned away, frightened by the vehemence of her emotion. (How lovely it would be to hurl the mixing bowl at Bridie. Lovelier still to see it hit her.)

'Veronica's just left.' Eleanor tried for neutral ground. 'She's taking it hard.'

'Ah, not so hard as poor Terence,' Bridie said.

'He's in a terrible state. But then, he would be—losing his wife like that.'

(It had been a mistake. There *was* no neutral ground with Bridie.)

'Is he still locked in his room?'

'He is that. *And* refusing to eat. I've been talking to him through the door.'

'I'm sure you've been a great comfort to him,' Eleanor said dryly.

'I've tried,' Bridie said. 'We've been praying together. I wanted him to come to church with Mam and me, but he won't leave his room.'

'He'll have to for the Inquest—and the funeral.' Eleanor hoped that she was right. Presumably, the police could force Terence to attend the Inquest, but if he then retreated back to his room and refused to emerge again for the funeral, the chances were very good that Veronica would have a permanent recluse on her hands for the rest of her life.

'That's as it may be,' Bridie said doubtfully. 'However, the Lord will provide.'

The trouble was that it was poor Veronica who would end up doing all of the providing. Eleanor wondered if Bridie could really be as pious—or obtuse—as she pretended.

'I want to go out, please,' Nicholas mumbled, sliding towards the back door.

'Oh, Nicholas!' Bridie stopped him with a reproachful look. 'Don't you want to come to church and pray for your poor Aunt Dee-Dee?'

'Uuuhh . . .' Nicholas wriggled in embarrassed horror, recognizing a question which was going to land him in trouble whether answered yes or no. He sent his mother an agonized glance.

Eleanor steadfastly went on chopping an onion, ignoring both Nicholas's anguish and Bridie's air of sly challenge. Whatever *she* said was going to be wrong, too. While Nicholas was learning other painful adult lessons, he might as well learn that there were situations when it was impossible to win. (And they seemed to have multiplied inordinately since Bridie had come.)

'Well . . . ?' Bridie stood waiting.

'I have to go and see Mickey Concannon right now.' Nicholas invoked the most telling force he knew. 'I *promised.*' He continued his interrupted progress towards the door and slid out like a blob of quicksilver, leaving behind only an impression of an apologetic smile.

'Ah, well.' *What else,* Bridie's intonation implied, *could you expect of a child being raised by a non-believer?*

Eleanor did not look up as a new disquiet filled her with foreboding. This was the first time Bridie had attempted to encroach on her authority. (If she continued to ignore it, would there be a full-fledged usurpation later?) Bridie obviously felt that she was acting from strength now. Death, like silence, was her dominion.

This time, however, the silence seemed to unnerve Bridie. 'I'll just get my things then,' she said. Eleanor nodded, still not looking up.

As the sound of Bridie's retreating footsteps faded down the hallway, two shining green eyes glittered in the shadows beneath the stove.

'You can come out now,' Eleanor said. 'It's all clear.'

Furface emerged cautiously, verifying the statement for herself. Before settling down to her milk again, she paused and gave Eleanor a long, reproachfully questioning look.

Eleanor tossed down her knife in exasperation. It was too much when even the cat was asking, *How much longer is she going to stay?*

'I don't know!' she stormed. 'I wish I *did* know. You needn't think I'm enjoying it any more than you—'

'Who are you talking—?' Kevin appeared in the

doorway. 'Oh!' He looked around. 'I thought there was someone out here. I heard you—'

'I was talking to Furface,' Eleanor said frostily.

'I see.' Kevin crossed to the fridge and began mixing himself a fresh drink. 'And what's *her* opinion?'

'She's not very happy. Your sister has upset her.'

'I see.' He did not have to ask which sister. He regarded Furface broodingly. She lifted her head and stared accusingly back. 'No, she doesn't look too happy.'

'She's *very* upset,' Eleanor emphasized.

'Well, if she should issue an ultimatum about choosing between her and Bridie—' Kevin stooped and stroked Furface absently—'for the love of God, choose her. She's a lot easier to get along with.'

'Nicholas is upset, too.' Eleanor would not be diverted. It was time they cleared the air on this subject.

'I know, I know.' Kevin straightened, rubbing his forehead wearily. 'For Christ's sake, let it be, Ellie. We'll deal with it later. After the funeral.'

'I'm sorry.' She was instantly contrite. 'It's just that—'

'I know.' He smiled at her weakly. 'You're fed up, too. So am I. We all are. But there's nothing can be done right this minute—' He broke off.

There were footsteps on the stairs. Eleanor turned towards the doorway as jumpily as Furface. Kevin caught his breath and they waited to see which way the footsteps would turn. After an endless hesitation, the front door opened softly and closed even more softly. Then there was silence.

'Trying to have a private conversation in this house is like a game of Russian Roulette!' Eleanor exploded. She did not want to pick a quarrel with Kevin at a time like this, but her pent-up fury demanded some release.

Furface looked from one to the other and prudently abandoned her milk, withdrawing under the stove once again.

'It's not *my* fault, Ellie,' Kevin defended.

'She's *your* sister!' Once again the accusation, irrefutable and irrational, sprang to her lips.

'They're *all* my sisters, Ellie,' Kevin said softly.

'Yes.' Eleanor found that if she said one more word, the tears would come. 'I'm sorry.' They came.

'Ellie, Ellie.' Kevin crossed to her and cradled her head on his shoulder. She knew instinctively that his own tears were close. 'Oh, Ellie. Life can be such hell.'

It was worse for Kevin but, while he was comforting her, he wasn't thinking of that. She allowed him the respite of worrying about her for a change and tugged at the handkerchief in his pocket.

'That's right,' he said. 'Have a good cry. You'll feel better.'

She was just snuggling in and seriously considering taking that advice when the doorbell rang.

'Now what?' Kevin moved away, his face dark with annoyance. 'Is it Bridie coming back for something she's forgotten?'

'Bridie has her own key,' Eleanor reminded him.

The doorbell rang again.

'Ah, Christ!' Kevin surrendered first and headed for the door; Eleanor followed him.

'Oh, it's you!' Kevin opened the door and fell back a step. 'What do you want?'

'I want to go back to the house to get my things.' James stepped into the hallway, forcing Kevin farther back. 'I want you to come with me.'

Eleanor placed her hand on Kevin's arm, cutting off what threatened to be a short sharp answer. She was shocked at James's appearance; he appeared to have deteriorated in just the short while since they had last seen him. It was not only the fact that he had not yet shaved, nor even the creases in his suit that seemed to have deepened and multiplied. Rather, it was the end-of-the-rope desperation quivering around him, the aura of utter despair emanating from nerve-ends beyond control—beyond hope.

(If it had been Kevin who had died so suddenly, so inexplicably, so uselessly, would *she* have disintegrated so swiftly and completely? Or would the need to sustain herself for the children have held her together? It was a question she did not wish to face. In any case, James and Dee-Dee had had no children—they had been at the beginning of their life together, with everything stretching out before them: home-making, children, love . . .)

'We were just going to have dinner, James,' she said softly. 'Come and have something to eat with us, then we'll go with you to get your things.'

'I'm not hungry,' James said.

'Then come and have a drink.' Throwing an arm around James's shoulders, Kevin manhandled him into the living-room.

Eleanor left them to it, frowning slightly when the size of the drink Kevin poured for James suggested that the main idea was less to sustain James than to render him unconscious.

'He's up to something,' Kevin said. 'He's got a shifty look in his eyes. I don't trust him.'

'Try to get him to the table.' Eleanor swiftly set another place. 'He'll collapse if he doesn't eat. He looks on the point of it now.'

'That might be the best thing that could happen,' Kevin said without hope. 'If he'd only collapse and stay collapsed right through the Inquest and until well after the funeral. We have enough problems without him going around stirring up more.'

18.

They stopped at Carmel's to thrust Nicholas and Margaret into the house. 'Just for half an hour,' Eleanor said hopefully. 'While we collect James's cases.' She dashed off quickly, while Carmel still had her mouth open to reply, and hurried across the street, catching up with Kevin and James.

'Come in.' Veronica opened the door with a harassed air. Her gaze lighted on James and her voice faltered. 'In there—' She gestured wearily towards the living-room. 'Everyone's in there. People have been telephoning—'

The telephone rang again and she broke off, hurrying towards it, but Bridie was already speaking into the receiver when they entered the room.

'Yes,' Bridie said. 'Oh yes, she's taking it very well, all things considered. Of course you can speak to her. Just one minute—'

Mam hurried to the phone as Bridie held it out to her. 'Ah, Mrs Concannon,' she said. 'Sure, it's good of you to ring . . . Yes. Yes, that was my Bridie, indeed. She's come home for her sister's funeral . . .'

So that was the story Mam had decided upon to save face. Behind Mam's back, Veronica made a small despairing gesture. Perhaps Mam believed it herself by this time. Bridie had come home for the funeral.

But, if Bridie hadn't come home, would there have been a funeral? If Bridie hadn't come home, would Dee-Dee still be alive? Was Bridie, directly or indirectly, the cause of it all?

Eleanor looked across the room at Bridie who was watching her mother, nodding and smiling, agreeing with everything she said. In time, would Bridie, too, come to believe that she had left the convent to attend her sister's funeral . . . and then just stayed on?

'My son-in-law?' Mam continued, rearranging the facts to suit herself. 'Ah, poor Terence is a broken man. Sure, your heart would bleed for him if you could see him. Just when she'd come back to him and they were going to work something out—'

James made a choked sound and Eleanor turned to see him staring incredulously at Mam. Nothing Dee-Dee could have told him would have prepared him for this. Even she, familiar as she was with Mam's ways, found it difficult to believe.

There was speculation, too, in James's gaze. No longer was he viewing Mam as the prospective mother-in-law to end all terrifying mothers-in-law; this time he was looking at her in the role of possible murderess.

In that role, Eleanor had to admit to herself, Mam stood out with spectacular qualifications. (Look at the way she had attempted to mastermind it with more subtle methods—as Carmel had borne witness.) It was not beyond reasonable doubt that Mam, having seen a sudden chance on the stairs to rid herself of a daughter who was an embarrassment, had taken it. Not that she could ever be brought to admit it—not even to herself. Oh no. Dee-Dee had tripped . . . or grown giddy . . . or fallen—and now was neatly boxed and about to be filed away where she could no longer cause any embarrassment by her ideas or actions. God moves in mysterious ways His wonders to perform. (And wasn't it a coincidence that His ways so neatly coincided with Mam's preferences?)

'That's right,' Mam continued blithely into the phone. 'We'll be waking her at O'Meara's. Yes . . . yes . . . Sure, that's very kind of you. We'll see you there, then. Thank you. God bless you.'

Mam hung up the receiver and went back to her chair. She had to pass James in order to do so. He stepped forward, but she walked past him as though he did not exist. In her eyes, he didn't. He was simply a ghost. A ghost out of Dee-Dee's past, and nothing to do with any of them.

'Mam—' Kevin attempted sternly to call her to order. 'Mam, here's James.'

'Oh yes?' Mam deliberately compounded the snub by not looking at him. 'What does *he* want? There's nothing for him here now.'

Eleanor caught her breath. (But why could such things still surprise her? Mam had always been callous to the point of brutality.)

'Mam!' Veronica protested. 'You can't—'

'It's all right,' James said swiftly. 'I only came to collect my things.'

'Oh yes,' Veronica said with relief. 'They're upstairs in your room. I—' She blushed so deeply it was painful to look at her. 'I'm afraid they're already packed.'

'That's right.' Mam smiled serenely into space. 'He's all ready to go.'

'He's not going far,' Kevin said. 'He's going to be at the wake with the rest of us. He's going to stand beside us where he belongs—as the man Dee-Dee was going to marry.'

'Never!' Mam snapped. 'Dee-Dee was already married. I'll not have that man standing there to advertise her sin to the world!'

'No wonder Dee-Dee left home,' James said flatly. 'She found no human warmth here.'

'Don't you dare speak to me like that, you—you heathen!' Mam rose out of her chair as though she would fly at him and demolish him. Shaking with rage, she seemed capable of any violence, ready to strike down anyone who stood in her pathway.

'Oh, James, sit down,' Veronica pleaded. 'Let me get you some tea—a drink—'

'You'd speak to a man like that—after he insulted your own mother?' Mam turned her fury on Veronica.

'Sometimes you need insulting!' Kevin jumped to the defence, although whether he was defending Veronica or James was not quite clear. 'Sometimes—'

'I'll just go upstairs and get my cases,' James said quietly. He did not seem displeased with the scene he had caused. (A few days ago, he would have been horrified. Was it the mark of his despair that he did not even seem to notice? Or was he noticing more than he seemed? There was a disquieting aura of satisfaction surrounding him, as though he had proved some point to himself.)

'No—' He halted Veronica as she stepped towards him. 'I'll go up by myself. I know the way.'

Veronica fell back, looking forlorn. If she couldn't be helpful, she was at a loss. She turned towards Mam, but Bridie was already there, bending over Mam solicitously, murmuring words of comfort, being the dutiful daughter.

Eleanor was conscious of James's footsteps moving down the hallway. There was a long pause when he must have reached the foot of the stairs. (Should one of them have gone with him, after all?) Then, slowly, he began to mount the stairs.

'Oh!' Veronica, too, was following the progress of those slow footsteps. Now they paused in the upstairs hallway. The tap on the door was so soft it might have gone unnoticed had some intuition not warned them that it was possible. There was the sound of his voice—urgent, but inaudible. Then an upstairs door opened and closed again.

'Oh no!' Veronica started forward frantically. 'He's gone in to Terence. They'll fight!'

'No, they won't, 'Ron.' Kevin caught her arm, holding her back. 'There's nothing for them to fight about . . . now.'

In the abrupt silence, there was a perfunctory ring of the doorbell, then the front door opened and Carmel was in their midst before anyone had had a chance to move.

'I came as soon as I could,' she said. 'I've left Pat with the kids—' She looked around curiously.

'James is upstairs,' Kevin said. 'With Terence.'

'Ooooh!' Carmel subsided into the nearest chair, catching the unspoken message. 'Then are they—?'

'We don't think they'll fight.' Eleanor cut her off before Mam and the others realized that that was the least of their worries. (If James told Terence his suspicions, and they decided to join forces—)

'You're still hanging on, are you?' Mam gave her bulging daughter-in-law a raking glance. 'It's being a long time coming. It isn't dead, is it?'

'Not the way it's kicking,' Carmel said sharply. 'It's just in no hurry to come out into *this* madhouse—and I can't say as I blame it!'

'Let me get you something,' Veronica placated hastily. 'A cup of tea or . . .' She trailed off, her heart not in it.

'Sit down, 'Ron,' Kevin said. 'We've just eaten. None of us wants anything.'

'Yes.' Veronica perched on the edge of a chair. She seemed to have developed a compulsive twitch. Her head kept jerking upwards and she frowned at the ceiling as though by the intensity of her concentration she could see through it to what was happening in the room upstairs.

'*I'd* like a cup of tea.' Mam was not trying to be kind

by giving Veronica something to do, she was trying to be difficult. And succeeding. Eleanor exchanged a glance of exasperation with Carmel.

'Yes, of course.' Veronica leaped up. 'I'll put the kettle on.'

'Sit down,' Kevin said. 'Bridie can do it. You won't mind, will you, Bridie? You can offer it up for something or other.'

'I'll be glad to,' Bridie said stiffly. 'All I ask is to be permitted to lighten Mam's burden.'

(Mam *had* no burdens, Mam *was* the burden. Veronica's burden, especially. If Bridie could be encouraged to take over a share, it would help Veronica enormously. If Veronica could only have more time to herself, time to develop outside interests of her own, perhaps some of the dreadful careworn look would fall away from her.)

'You're a good girl, Bridie,' Mam said pointedly.

Veronica sank back into her chair and stared upwards again. There was total silence upstairs. (What had they expected—shouts? Blows? Breaking furniture? As Kevin had said, there was nothing for Terence and James to fight about now.)

'I'll make enough for all of us,' Bridie smirked. 'The others may change their minds once it's made.' She bustled off to the kitchen.

'It would choke me,' Carmel muttered. 'If she didn't poison it, anyway, that is.'

'You've no call to talk that way,' Mam snapped. 'Bridie is a Woman of God.'

'*Was*,' Carmel reminded her gleefully. 'She's just one of the rest of us poor bastards now.'

'You're probably delirious.' Infuriatingly, Mam forgave her. 'I wouldn't be surprised if the baby arrives this very night.'

'If it does, I'll know who to blame!' Carmel's colour had risen with her temper, making it look possible that Mam's prophecy would come true.

'Take it easy,' Kevin counselled, with the abstracted look of one mentally counting off months. 'Don't get yourself all excited. It isn't good for you.'

'Are you all right?' Veronica was out of her chair again. 'Shall I get you—?'

'For the love of God, sit down!' Kevin roared. 'You'll drive us all crazy with your fussing around. Carmel is perfectly all right. You are, aren't you?' he added cautiously to Carmel

'Of course I am,' Carmel said. She settled back in her chair and did some deep breathing. 'You know I never have any trouble with birthing.'

'There's always a first time,' Mam said hopefully. 'And you're not as young as you used to be.'

'You keep quiet,' Kevin warned. 'We've had just about enough from you.'

'A fine way to talk to your own—' Mam broke off, looking beyond them to the doorway.

In the incipient family battle, they had not heard the sounds of anyone descending the stairs. Now Terence and James paused in the doorway before advancing into the room.

'Terence!' This time, Veronica was on her feet to stay. 'Terence—' She started towards him, but something in his face halted her and she fell back. 'Terence, what's the matter?'

He didn't answer. With James close at his heels, Terence strode into the centre of the room and turned to survey the others. His face was grim.

For the first time, Eleanor knew fear. She realized that the emotions besetting her earlier had merely been counterfeits of fear. She could now recognize them as unhappiness, disquiet, uneasiness—dread, even. But not fear. The fear had surfaced now and there was no mistaking it this time.

'Ah, Terence.' Bridie came back into the room carrying a tray of tea-things. 'You've come down.

That's very wise of you. You'll have a cup of tea, won't you?'

'No.' He looked at her sharply, suspiciously. 'I'll never eat or drink a thing under this roof again.'

'Terence—' Now even Bridie realized there was something amiss. 'Whatever's the matter with you?'

'The matter—' Terence stared at her incredulously. 'The matter? Dee-Dee's dead! Don't you realize that? Is it nothing to you?' He answered his own question. 'No, I don't suppose it is.'

'We're all going to die some time,' Bridie said calmly. 'So where's the fuss? Dee-Dee has just gone home to God a bit earlier than the rest of us, and she will live in the light of His countenance . . .' (Trust Bridie to spoil it) '. . . eventually.'

'Eventually—!' Terence choked.

'You know as well as I do—' Bridie faced him implacably—'that she'll at the least have a long, long spell in Purgatory to pay—' her eyes slid across James—'for what she's done.'

'Oh Christ!' Carmel muttered. She shivered abruptly, although her face was glistening with a sudden thin film of perspiration.

'Are you all right?' Eleanor moved swiftly to her side. The others, intent on Terence and Bridie, appeared not to have noticed. 'It's not the baby coming?'

'If I have anything to say about it, it is.' Carmel huddled forward, grimly straining. 'Begod, all I want right now is a nice quiet week in hospital away from all this mess.'

'You were always jealous of her, weren't you, Bridie?' Terence's voice was dispassionate. 'Because she was all that you never had it in you to be.'

There was murder in the flash of Bridie's eyes before she lowered her gaze in that irritating parade of Christian humility. (Which somehow always rang false—the murder seemed far more natural.)

'Terence!' For once, Veronica was too shocked to be placating. 'You're drunk!'

'I'm not. But, if I were, haven't I a right to be?' Terence swung on her. 'You're another one, Veronica.' He turned to Mam. 'I don't know what you did to them. I don't know how you brought them up, but they're all less than human. All except Dee-Dee—and you fixed her, too, finally, didn't you? You got rid of her.'

'Terence—' Mam's voice was thunderous. 'Go to your room!'

'Ah, no.' Terence shook his head. 'No. That doesn't work with me. I'm no blood of yours—thank God. I'm nothing to you—and you're nothing to me. I'll see you in hell—or in jail—and glad of it!'

'That's enough of that, Terence.' Kevin moved forward. 'Let's go back upstairs now.'

'He's all right.' James moved to block Kevin.

'I see.' Kevin looked at James, his gaze becoming actively hostile. 'I might have known you put him up to this.'

'He put me up to nothing,' Terence said. 'Do you think *I* didn't hear what Dee-Dee said? Do you think I wouldn't remember her last words? Do you think I haven't been sitting up there running through that whole scene over and over in my mind, trying to place who was where?'

'Terence—' Veronica whimpered. 'Don't—'

'Take him away from here,' Mam ordered. 'He's gone mad. I won't have him in the house any longer.'

'You'd like that, wouldn't you?' Terence turned to her slowly. 'That would suit you right down to the ground. That's the way you've operated all your life. You got rid of anyone who didn't agree with you.'

This time Mam looked frightened. As though she realized she had set in motion a force she could no longer control. But how long ago had she set it in motion? Back when she first married him off to

Dee-Dee? Or when she persuaded him to take up permanent residence in her home and await Dee-Dee's return?

'Come on . . . baby . . .' Carmel murmured. 'Do your . . . mother . . . a favour . . .'

'Carmel,' Eleanor whispered anxiously. 'Do you think you ought?'

'Look at . . . the alternative . . .' Carmel continued her breathing exercises.

Eleanor looked—and decided to accompany Carmel to the hospital. Perhaps it was too much to hope that the sudden advent of Carmel's baby would halt this nightmare, but it might allow the two of them to escape. (The better to pick up the pieces later?)

'You're right,' she encouraged. 'Keep trying.'

Mam and Bridie stood together now—defiant—realizing everything Terence was accusing them of and defying them to prove it—or even to dare to put it into cold hard words. Before their implacable faces, Terence had faltered to a stop. He had acceded to Mam's domination for too long to lightly overthrow it.

They had obviously counted on that. (Was it possible that they did not understand the scope and depth of the pain that had been caused? Of the hurt that would not ease?) Certainly they were standing there calmly, smugly, even—awaiting the usual end of a family quarrel when a man found his womenfolk solidly ranged against him: when the man would mutter a curse and fling himself off to the nearest pub, not to be seen sober again until the whole thing had blown over. (Did they imagine that this would blow over?)

'Neither of us are leaving this house.' They had reckoned without James. 'Not until we get some answers.'

'And what will you do with the answers?' Kevin asked.

'I don't know yet,' James admitted.

'Oh, make them stop—' Veronica drifted closer to Kevin. 'Make them stop,' she pleaded.

'I'm sorry, Veronica,' Terence said. 'I don't want to upset anybody, but isn't it better that we know the truth?'

'Upset anybody—' Veronica's laugh was faintly hysterical.

'One of you—' James moved to stand beside Terence, facing Mam and Bridie squarely. 'One of you pushed Dee-Dee.'

'That isn't true.' Bridie's eyes gleamed dangerously. (If James were at the head of a flight of stairs right now, it would not be safe for him to turn his back on Bridie.)

'One of you . . .' Terence echoed with less conviction. (He had lived with these people for ten years, it wasn't so academic to him. Perhaps he was beginning to wonder what good it would do, what further steps James might try to force him to take.)

'You might as well admit it—' James looked from Mam to Bridie and back again. 'We're going to stand here until you do.'

'Ah, God!' Mam clutched at her heart, gasping, playing the card that had never failed her. 'It's an attack coming on. I've got to lie down.' She started for the door.

'Yes. I thought it was you.' James blocked her way. 'You pushed her around all her life, didn't you? You pushed all of them around. What was one more push?'

'For the love of God,' Bridie said, 'let her past—'

'Ever since I've been here,' James said bitterly, 'I've noticed that everyone talks about the love of God—but not one of you ever had any love for each other.'

'Get out of the way.' There were tears in Bridie's eyes as she tried to support Mam's tottering bulk and move past James.

'Ah, Christ!' Terence gave up. 'Let her go!' He pulled James out of the way.

'You'll let her go—?' James asked incredulously. 'Just like that?'

'What does it matter?' Terence turned away. 'Dee-Dee's dead. Nothing's going to bring her back. Where's the sense of all this? She's gone.'

'Thank heavens,' Eleanor murmured. There was more to it than that, she sensed. Terence wasn't just giving up the quest for revenge James had pushed him into, he was giving up Dee-Dee. Or perhaps admitting to himself at last that he had never really had her.

'You needn't worry—' Terence spoke to Mam's retreating back—'I'll be getting out of this house. Nothing on earth could make me stay in it now.'

'Terence—no!' Veronica protested. 'Mam was just upset. She didn't mean it. This is your home—'

'That's nice of you, Veronica.' Terence forced his features into a smile. 'You've always been very nice—too nice for this family. But you do understand, don't you? There's nothing left for me here. I've been thinking it over and I've made my decision. I'm going to emigrate.'

'No!' Veronica whispered, as though in deep pain. 'No, Terence, no!'

'Oh, not till after the funeral,' he assured her. 'Don't worry, I'll observe the proprieties. But as soon as ever it's over, I'm off. Canada, I think. Get off into the wilds all by myself. Start a new life.'

'Then it was all for nothing,' Veronica murmured to herself, so softly they barely heard her.

'What's that?' James was instantly alert. He advanced upon her, but she had eyes only for Terence.

Mam and Bridie halted just short of the doorway and turned slowly.

'Not *you*,' James protested incredulously.

'*Her*?' Terence snapped to full attention. 'Never! You're mad!'

'Oh, Terence,' Veronica said sorrowfully, 'you'll never understand, will you? I was never alive to you, was I? Not really. You hardly knew I was here. I realized that, but I kept hoping—'

'Never!' Terence continued to deny the evidence of his own ears. 'Not *you*.'

'Then *she* came back.' Veronica tried earnestly to explain. 'When she wrote she wanted to come for a visit, I invited her to stay here. I thought seeing her again might break the spell for you. Especially if you saw her happy and in love with another man. But it didn't work that way. You still wouldn't accept it. I think I knew then that there was no future for me—ever.'

'Veronica—' Kevin warned—'stop talking now. That's enough. You're tired and upset. You've having some kind of breakdown. You don't really know what you're saying.'

'It was an accident, really,' Veronica said. 'I didn't mean to harm her. I just wanted to get her out of the way for a while. Didn't you *hear* the things she was saying? All those awful things she kept saying?'

'Veronica, it isn't true.' Terence was shaken to the core. 'It can't be true—'

'She kept pushing you at Bridie. She kept saying now that Bridie was back, you ought to marry *her*— the way you intended to do in the beginning. If she kept on saying it often enough, you might have done it. Because you always did whatever she told you to. Always—'

'Christ!' Terence stared at her, aghast, perhaps remembering all the little signposts he had plunged past unwittingly: the extra work Veronica had done for him, the little marks of special favour, the mute pleas for attention . . . for love.

'I was never there for you at all, was I? Not that

way.' Veronica's voice was a thin forlorn thread of pain. 'No one ever thought about me—'

'Veronica—' Terence started towards her, perhaps he didn't know himself what he was going to do.

'No!' she screamed. 'Don't come near me! Don't look at me like that—' She turned and ran from the room.

They stood frozen as the front door slammed. They still had not begun to move when they heard the sharp sudden squeal of brakes outside and then a curious hollow thud.

'Christ!' Kevin charged for the door.

Mam gave a faint whimper and slumped to the floor.

Carmel surged to her feet then, with a sudden convulsion of her body, fell back in her chair. 'Begod!' she said. 'Here it comes!'

Eleanor hurried to the telephone and began dialling for an ambulance, perhaps two ambulances.

'Veronica—' James was still incredulous, almost indignant. 'But I *liked* her.' Eleanor noted that, for him, Veronica had already slipped into the past tense. 'I really *liked* her.'

'We *still* do,' Eleanor said sadly.

19.

Things looked better in the morning only because they could not possibly have become worse. Veronica had not survived the night. Mam had.

Eleanor stopped in at the Maternity Ward before leaving the hospital to visit Carmel and her new son.

'They say Mam will never be the same woman again,' Eleanor told her.

'Thank Christ for that!' Carmel blinked sleepily, still groggy from the anaesthetic. 'Did you hear the good news about me? I've had the most wonderful stroke of luck!' Her eyes brightened. 'I nearly died and they had to give me a hysterectomy. Do you realize what that means? This little one really *is* the end of the line. I can buy real clothes—dresses that aren't tents. I can make plans ahead, accept invitations and know I'll be feeling all right when the time comes to go. I can book holidays months in advance. I can begin living!'

'I'm so pleased for you,' Eleanor said. (Life and death, intertwined, going on.)

'I'm glad it was a boy,' Carmel said. 'If it was a girl, I'd have had to name her after her aunts, and it would always be there to remind us, so to speak. It's better this way. I wanted to call him Finis—but it's not a proper name, so I suppose we'll have to settle for Fingal, as the closest we can get.' She yawned.

'Begod, I'm exhausted. But that's another good thing . . .' her voice began to trail off sleepily. 'I'll never be *this* exhausted again.'

The telephone rang as Eleanor entered the house. She picked it up automatically and was appalled to discover Mrs Concannon, quivering with curiosity, at the other end of the line. After the night she had been through, it was more than she could cope with.

'Yes, Mrs Concannon,' she agreed weakly, wondering if she had the courage to disconnect her. 'It was a terrible tragedy. I—I don't know—'

'Here—' Bridie came down the stairs and took the telephone away from her.

'Mrs Concannon, it it? Yes, this is Bridie . . . Yes, a terrible thing . . . We must trust in God's mercy, that's all . . .'

Kevin came out of the kitchen slowly and stood staring at Bridie.

'It was the suddenness of it,' Bridie went on. 'There we were, just sitting there talking. Then Carmel started the baby. We couldn't get through on the telephone and Veronica ran out to get help. It wasn't really anybody's fault. She didn't look where she was going and the driver couldn't stop in time when she ran between two cars. It was God's will, that's all . . .'

Eleanor and Kevin moved together, still watching— and listening to—Bridie in astonishment. She sent them a placid smile.

'Poor Mam . . . yes, it was very hard on her. She took a shock, like, along with her heart. But, glory be to God, she's going to get better. No . . . no, I won't be going back to the convent. Someone will have to take care of Mam . . . Ah, no . . . it's no more than my duty . . . Yes. Yes, it will be a double funeral now. It will be better to get it all over with at once. Less strain on Mam and the family . . .'

Still smiling, still calm and completely in control, Bridie ended the conversation and hung up.

'I never thought—' Kevin said in awe—'you could lie so well, Bridie.'

'Ah, no,' Bridie protested. 'It wasn't lying. Not really. It was just rearranging the facts a little. It's so much more natural for everything to have happened that way, don't you agree? And, if we all keep to the same story, there's no reason why anyone should ever think different.'

'Well, Bridie,' Kevin said. 'It appears that you have your uses, after all.' It was a pretty tattered and storm-beaten one, but it was an olive branch.

'I'll be moving up to the house,' Bridie said. 'But, if you don't mind, I'll stay here just a bit longer—until Mam gets out of the hospital.' She blushed. 'I can't go yet—I'd be there alone with Terence. It wouldn't be proper.'

'That's quite all right, Bridie,' Kevin said gravely. 'We wouldn't want poor Terence tempted beyond his strength.'

'Then I'll get off to the hospital now and make sure Mam is comfortable.'

Bridie nearly collided with Nicholas, rushing through the doorway. Abruptly subdued, he glanced at his parents and almost tiptoed into the hallway. Deprived once more of an opportunity to speak in privacy, Eleanor and Kevin exchanged helpless glances.

'Well . . .' Kevin stared down at his son, trying, with an almost audible shifting of mental gears, to make suitable conversation. 'Decided to come home, have you?'

'I've been over to Mickey Concannon's,' Nicholas said. 'His mother gave us breakfast.' (Thank heavens Nicholas didn't know anything worth pumping for.)

'Fine,' Kevin said abstractedly. 'That's good.'

'Mickey Concannon says things always happen in threes—' Nicholas rushed to share his newly-acquired information. 'He says we've had our three now, so everything should be all right again. And he says—' he hesitated. 'He says, even if Aunt Veronica couldn't talk, the priest was there and so it was all right— Mickey Concannon says—'

'And did Mickey Concannon tell you—' Eleanor broke in with asperity—'that Protestants eat their children?'

'No-o-o . . .' Nicholas looked at her uncertainly, his eyes wide. (She shouldn't have said it. She shouldn't have let Mickey Concannon's nonsense annoy her so much. Heaven knew what traumas—)

'No!' Nicholas shouted with sudden laughter. 'That's just what stupid old Mickey Concannon *would* believe! He'd think it was true!'

So, no traumas. And it appeared that the reign of Mickey Concannon was over, his sway had been broken.

'And we'll eat you, too!' Furface had strolled into the hallway to see what was going on. Nicholas made a sudden dive at her. 'We'll eat you with sugar and cream!'

Catching his mood, Furface gave a skittish yowl and bounded away, Nicholas in laughing pursuit. They thundered towards the kitchen.

Eleanor sighed faintly and Kevin looked at her. 'You're tired,' he said. 'You ought to lie down—get some rest, even if you can't sleep.'

'So ought you.' She sighed again, thinking of Veronica.

'I know,' Kevin said. 'It doesn't seem right, but what would you have? 'Ron's gone, too, now. It wouldn't do any good to let it all come out. The rest of us have to go on living here.'

'I suppose so. But what will happen now about the Inquest?'

'They have a fair amount of leeway and can use their own discretion in cases like this,' Kevin said. 'I don't think we need worry too much. They aren't out to pillory innocent families. They'll keep to the surface of things and will probably bring in either an open verdict or an accident verdict on both of them.'

'And James—' Eleanor tried not to sound bitter. 'Will James be satisfied with that?'

'James and I have had a little talk,' Kevin's face was grim. 'He isn't going to raise any awkward points. He's quite reasonable about it—now. It's almost too much for him, realizing what he's done. All things considered, he's decided not to stay for the funeral. He wants to go home as soon as the Inquest is over. And nobody's going to argue with him about that decision.'

'Then there'll just be Terence as chief mourner at the funeral, after all.' Eleanor smiled faintly. 'The correct Catholic proprieties will be observed.'

'The irony is Mam won't be there to see them,' Kevin agreed. 'She'll probably have to stay in hospital another two or three weeks.'

'Mam . . . ,' Eleanor said thoughtfully. Mam was the cause of it all, really. Mam, who had kept Veronica from making any life of her own. How much had Mam known? Had she deliberately encouraged Terence to live with them because she knew that would keep Veronica at home? Veronica, who ministered to her comfort, to Terence's comfort, and had so little life of her own. And that little so wasted. Eleanor shuddered.

'Ellie—' Kevin was watching her. 'Will you hate it so much? Going on living here, I mean? Would you rather move away? I could find a job somewhere else—'

'No.' That wouldn't erase the memories. And she

would miss Carmel and Pat and the kids. Even Bridie looked as though she might shape up now that she had definite responsibilities. (It was doubtful that they would ever become bosom friends, but they would get along.) And it wouldn't do to uproot Nicholas.

'No,' she sighed, turning towards the stairs. 'It's just—'

'Yes?' Kevin encouraged.

'It's just that I've decided—' she smiled weakly— 'next time round, I'm going to marry an orphaned atheist with no relatives whatever.'

'There's a coincidence.' Kevin put his arm around her waist. 'Next time round, I plan to *be* an orphaned atheist with not a relative to my name.'

Leaning against each other, they ascended the stairs slowly.

ABOUT THE AUTHOR

Marian Babson is the author of more than twenty-five mysteries. Winner of the Poisoned Chalice and Sleuth awards, she was also a nominee for the British Gold and Silver Dagger awards. She is listed in *Publishers Weekly* as one of today's best British mystery writers. She lives in London.

If you enjoyed *Untimely Guest,* you'll want to read Marian Babson's next mystery, *In the Teeth of Adversity,* coming soon from Bantam.

The following is a preview of that title.

Simple things amuse simple minds. I was deriving quite a bit of amusement from the early edition of the evening paper. I had just made a note of the rapidly rising actress on page seven, who had been photographed against the background of her antique silver collection, holding the prize piece of carved jade from her treasury of objets d'art, and captioned by a melancholy quote saying how much she was going to miss her little mews cottage and her treasures during the next three months when she would be filming in Spain. I underscored her name and made a notation to get in touch with her after the burglary, when she would be looking for another—and brighter—public relations person.

"Stop that!" I shouted as a bandit-masked whirlwind sprang from an ambush of late-afternoon shadows and hurled herself at my Biro. Capturing it successfully, she tumbled over and over across the desk, kicking at it with her hind legs and uttering loud yowls of defiance.

You had to laugh at the little clown. A fact she constantly used against me. "Behave yourself." I tried to recapture the Biro, but she rolled away from me with it, growling as though she really meant it. Only the rakish tilt of her ears betrayed her playfulness.

"Come on, give it back." I feinted for it again, and her tail lashed menacingly, her slanted blue eyes glittering. She was having a lovely time.

"Be a good cat," I said. I had dropped the paper by now and she had my full attention. Which was what she'd wanted all along.

Suddenly, she abandoned the game. The Biro dropped from her mouth and rolled across the desk unnoticed. She was taut and alert, blue eyes staring at the door. I followed her look, seeing nothing but the closed door. After a moment, though, I heard it, too.

Someone was taking the stairs two at a time. Someone gained the tiny hallway and pounded on the door, but didn't wait for any social niceties like being invited to enter. He burst through the door, slamming it behind him and leaning against it, looking around wildly, gasping for breath. His eyes were bulging, his face purple, but he was just recognizable—the white coat helped.

I gazed at him in mild amusement. True, I was three or four months overdue for my semiannual checkup, but you don't really expect your dentist to get *emotional* over a fact like that. Particularly, as Gerry and I were practically the only National Health patients he had on his eminent and star-studded roster of Famous Mouths I Have Looked Into.

"You've got to help me," he choked. "You've got to help me, *now*. Quickly!"

It was a good line, and probably one he had picked up from patients ringing in the middle of the night with throbbing abcesses. But it seemed to be slightly misdirected.

"Are you sure you have the right place?" That was as near as I dared get to asking him if he knew where he was. "This is Perkins and Tate—"

"Public Relations, Limited," he finished for me. "Of course, it's the right place. Public relations—that's what I need right now. God!— How I need public relations!"

It was a statement to warm the cockles of many a heart at the Institute of Public Relations, but it simply made *my* blood run cold. I mean, public relations isn't usually something you need immediately, like a fix, or a stiff drink. If you do, it means the horse has bolted, the barn has burned to the ground, the ground has caved into a previously unsuspected mineshaft, and somebody is handing you a rusty heap and demanding that you put it all back the way it was.

Pandora glared at him, twitching her nose, then abruptly dived under the desk, hissing. She had recently had the last of her booster shots, and men in white jackets smelling, however faintly, of antiseptic were at the top of her Hate Parade.

He ignored her; I doubt that he even noticed her. He was still staring wildly in my general direction, waiting for me to wave the magic wand and make everything all right again.

"Why don't you sit down, and we'll talk this over," I suggested.

"Sit down? We haven't time! We've got to get into action now, you fool! Don't you understand? She's dead. Morgana Fane! She died under the anaesthetic in *my* dental chair. My God! *Morgana Fane!*"

I instantly needed a stiff drink myself. Morgana Fane—the Model of the Moment—of this decade. About to be the Bride of the Year. That mesmeric face, which had decorated a thousand magazine covers, launched a thousand styles, and—it was rumoured in the peephole press— shipwrecked a few dozen marriages, now stilled forever. It was the end of an Era.

Fortunately, the company was fairly solvent at the moment, and there was a bottle of Scotch in the kitchen cupboard. Going for it, I asked, "What did the police say about it?"

"I haven't called them!" He was affronted. "Not yet. That's why I came to you. I want a press representative with me before I do."

Oh, fine. At the rate he was going, a solicitor would be more help when the police arrived. They were not going to take kindly to playing second fiddle to a public relations man. Although I appreciated the good dentist's problem. A society/show business practice, of the kind he had built up, depends on word-of-mouth recommendations and confidence. Lots of confidence. He could go out of style as fast as an old-fashioned abortionist if the death of a famous patient wasn't handled properly. Faster. And Morgana Fane—I found myself echoing the dentist—my God!

"Didn't she respond at all to the kiss of life?" I turned just in time to catch the shifty look that flashed across his face. He hadn't bothered to try. He'd been too worried about his own skin. He'd flown for a press representative—probably leaving her still there in the chair. *That* would look great in the headlines.

I took the drink I had poured for him and put it back in the cupboard beside the bottle—Gerry could drink it later. We were going to have enough problems without our dentist facing the music with liquor on his breath. It would be all the press needed—and I didn't think the police would react too favourably to it, either.

"There was no point in trying," he defended hastily, having evidently caught the look that flashed across *my* face just before I turned away. "Any fool could tell that she was gone."

There was a steady hissing sound emanating from beneath the desk. I just looked at him, my face as blank as I could possibly make it. I felt like joining Pandora under the desk for a hissing session, but it was a luxury I was denied.

This expensive dentist had not carried Perkins & Tate (Public Relations) Ltd. on his National Health books just because he could not resist our winsome faces. It was one of those tacit understandings, and Gerry and I had dutifully seen to it that his name was planted in a few columns and the discreet mention was inserted wherever possible. Very discreet—the dental profession being as twitchy as the medical on the subject of publicity. It had worked quite well and to our mutual satisfaction for several years. This time, however, the piper was really presenting the bill—and with a vengeance.

"She's still there," I said flatly. Just checking, I didn't expect any contradiction.

I didn't get one. "Right where she expired," he said. His face twitched with indignation. "In *my* dental chair!" He made it sound as though the only decent thing she could have done was to crawl into an anonymous gutter to die.

"What about your nurse?"

"She wasn't there today. Fortunately, she has the flu." It was obvious that he was grateful for a woman with some grasp of fundamental decencies.

"Does anyone know you've come here?" That was the first thing. If we could cover his tracks to Perkins & Tate, we might have a chance of retrieving the situation.

"I didn't tell anyone—if that's what you mean. And no one saw me leave the office."

That checked out. The reception and waiting rooms were on the ground floor, the torture chambers were upstairs. The front door opened into the hallway and faced the stairs, you had to detour through a door on the left into the reception area and the waiting room. The nurse notified you when your number had come up, and with a brave smile, you went through the door and up the stairs to whatever doom awaited you. The door was always closed, presumably so that the nervous clientele in the waiting room couldn't see the victims staggering out after they had been worked on.

Since Endicott Zayle hadn't had the bad luck to encounter someone actually entering as he was slipping out, he would not have been seen. If we could get him back in again without being seen, there might be a fighting chance.

"When did this happen?"

He seemed calmer, now that he had thrown the burden on someone else's shoulders. "About ten minutes ago."

That wasn't so bad. If he'd had to go and call in the wrong people, at least he hadn't let any grass grow under his feet about it. He didn't seem wholly aware of the enormity of what he had done, or how it would sound if the papers got hold of it. He was too concerned with the fact of her death to consider his own desertion of her.

"How did you get here?"

"I took a taxi."

He must have been fairly conspicuous in that white jacket. Could we take a chance that no taxi driver would remember? Even a doctor on the most urgent emergency call would throw on a coat before going out in weather like this. But taxi drivers, as a whole, are the most sophisticated social group in England, as well as the most discreet. With good reason— if they told all they knew, a few bastions of our society would crumble, and we don't have all that many left.

"You didn't do anything silly"—it was better to find out the worst right away—"like keeping the taxi waiting, did you?"

"Certainly not." He bristled. "I realize it

wouldn't look too well if the police discovered I came to you before I called them."

It would look bloody awful, but I was relieved to find he had some inkling of the fact.

"Naturally, I've prepared a story in advance," he said. "In case they find out."

This cheered me a bit more. Perhaps he was brighter than he had previously given indication of being. "What story?" I asked hopefully.

"I shall say"—a crafty light glittered in the depths of his tiny eyes—"Everything Went Black. And when I came to, I was here." He waited triumphantly for my applause.

I looked at him bleakly. To get away with that one, you have to be 36-22-34 and preferably blond. At 44-52-58 and going bald, it just wasn't on. I tried to break it to him gently. "That one went out with 'I didn't know the gun was loaded.'"

He bristled, about to take umbrage again, when the steady hissing sound from under the desk unnerved him. "What's that?" He looked around uneasily. "Is something going to explode?"

"Only the cat," I said.

"Cat?" Locating the source of the sound, he crouched to look under the desk.

Lashing her tail, Pandora retreated, switching from a hiss to a growl. She knew his sort, she informed him. They petted you and chucked you under the chin and called you sweet names, and just when you were preening yourself that you'd made a new conquest, they jabbed a dirty great needle into your rump.

"I don't think she likes me," he said.

"She's shy," I said. "Don't worry about her." It seemed superfluous to tell him to worry about himself, it was amazing that anything could distract him from that absorbing concern.

He and Pandora continued staring at each other, which, ordinarily, would have been all right. However, it was wasting time, and back at the surgery, his partner, a restless patient, or even a just-recovered nurse might open the door to his office and discover the Corpse of the Year—with the dentist gone missing. Even the most loyal partner might be forgiven for jumping to conclusions under those circumstances—not to mention the police.

"Look," I said. "The best thing for you to do is get straight back to your surgery and call the police. Take my coat—you're pretty conspicuous in that white jacket—I'll pick it up later. I'll follow along right behind you. Then if the police question my presence, I'll say I had a sudden toothache and dropped in for emergency treatment." It might not be the best story in the world, but it was several cuts above his. And I might be able to knock together a better one between now and the time the question actually came up.

He didn't move.

"Hurry up," I urged. How long did it take a body to cool? Long enough for the police to detect the length of time between death and the time they were called in? "We haven't much time."

"I—I haven't told you everything—yet," he said. He seemed more interested in gazing into

Pandora's eyes—however baleful—than in looking up and meeting mine. "You don't know the worst."

I usually don't. "Go ahead," I said grimly. "Surprise me."

"Morgana is—was—desperately afraid of hypodermics. I did everything to try to save that tooth—I've babied it along for years. But it was no use anymore. And she'd never had a tooth out before. The very thought made her hysterical. I assured her that the extraction was necessary, but she'd worked herself up into such a state—"

He still hadn't looked away from Pandora. She was working herself up into quite a state, too. "Go on," I said.

"Well, Tyler Meredith—my partner—has been developing a new anaesthetic. A gas type. He's worked on it for a long time, with very good results. We thought . . ."

I began to see where this was leading, but I didn't want to believe it. I closed my eyes and hoped that, when I opened them again, the nightmare would have run its course.

It hadn't. He was still there, still staring into Pandora's eyes, still babbling on.

". . . I can't understand it. We had such wonderful results with the laboratory animals—"

"Just let me get this straight," I interposed weakly. "You mean that you used *Morgana Fane* as a guinea pig for an untried anaesthetic?"

Experience Murder Most British with Marian Babson

Murder at the Cat Show

A glorified cat show is about to become an exhibition of grand larceny, catnapping, and murder.

❑ 28590-4 $3.95

Murder Sails at Midnight

Four wealthy women sail from New York to Genoa aboard an Italian luxury liner. As the passengers frolic in the sumptuous elegance of her staterooms and cabarets, a killer stalks the decks under a full moon.

❑ 28096-1 $3.50

Tourists are for Trapping

A luxury tour with a premium price tag. Now conspiracy, perjury, and murder have just been added to the itinerary.

❑ 29031-2 $3.99

BANTAM OFFERS THE FINEST IN CLASSIC AND MODERN BRITISH MURDER MYSTERIES

Dorothy Cannell
- ❑ *The Widows Club*   27794-4 $3.95
- ❑ *Down the Garden Path*   26895-3 $3.95
- ❑ *Mum's the Word*   28686-2 $4.99

Michael Dibdin
- ❑ *Ratking*   28237-9 $4.99

Colin Dexter
- ❑ *The Dead of Jericho*   27237-3 $3.95
- ❑ *Last Bus to Woodstock*   27777-4 $3.95
- ❑ *Last Seen Wearing*   28003-1 $3.95
- ❑ *The Riddle of the Third Mile*   27363-9 $4.50
- ❑ *The Silent World of Nicholas Quinn*   27238-1 $3.95
- ❑ *Service of All the Dead*   27239-X $3.95
- ❑ *The Secret of Annex 3*   27549-6 $3.95

Dorothy Simpson
- ❑ *Close Her Eyes*   18518-7 $2.25
- ❑ *Dead by Morning*   28606-4 $3.95
- ❑ *Dead on Arrival*   27000-1 $3.50
- ❑ *Element of Doubt*   28175-5 $3.50
- ❑ *Last Seen Alive*   27773-1 $3.95
- ❑ *Night She Died*   27772-3 $3.50
- ❑ *Puppet for a Corpse*   27774-X $3.95
- ❑ *Six Feet Under*   25192-9 $3.95
- ❑ *Suspicious Death*   28459-2 $3.95

Available at your local bookstore or use this page to order.

Send to: Bantam Books, Dept. MC 6
            414 East Golf Road
            Des Plaines, IL 60016

Please send me the items I have checked above. I am enclosing
$_____ (please add $2.50 to cover postage and handling).
Send check or money order, no cash or C.O.D.'s, please.

Mr/Ms._____

Address_____

City/State_____Zip_____

Please allow four to six weeks for delivery.
Prices and availability subject to change without notice.   MC6 11/91